The Other Side Of The River

Sandra Allensworth

Published by Sandra Allensworth, 2023.

THE OTHER SIDE OF THE RIVER

First edition. February 4, 2023.

Written by Sandra Allensworth.

To Eva and the Joy Writers who understand the need to write and to my family and friends who do not but encouraged me anyway. To Tracy for her patience and technical advice and most of all to my Heavenly Father who gave me a small gift with words.

Chapter 1
The Racetrack
May 2012

Carolina watched patiently as the elderly couple settled themselves into the old blue Chevy. The familiar gray cloud of loneliness hovered over her as she watched the woman's face crinkle into a tender smile, gazing into the lined brown face of her companion. He reached over and stroked her cheek before putting the car in gear. *Did Darren ever look at me like that?* The old man peered over his shoulder before backing out of the parking space, raising his hand in salute to Carolina.

Pulling into the vacated space, she was thankful that she wouldn't have far to walk to the racetrack. It was only May, but the heat was already promising a hot, dry summer. *Too much time in the classroom*, she thought. *I must be getting soft, or,* she smiled wryly to herself, *old.* Carolina was in the middle of finals week and the students weren't any happier than she was to be confined in the classroom. Their spring fever and tension over the final tests made her edgy. She was up for tenure and although this was what she had worked so hard to attain, the commitment, the monotony stretching on for years to come, was weighing heavily on her mind. Checking to be sure that she had her keys, lip balm and money in hand, she shoved everything into her pockets and shut the pickup door with one efficient motion.

As Carolina made her way across the parking lot and walked down the long decline to the racetrack, she looked up at the dry hills. No small wonder that the fire warning on the road up here had read, "Fire Danger—HIGH." She took a deep breath, trying to catch the scent of the pines. There was none. She missed that. Too many people and cars, not enough rain. The forest-unhealthy. There was only a dry, dusty smell. It used to cloud up and rain almost every afternoon when she was a kid. She loved to come up here with her dad. He taught her the differences between running horses and working horses, between Quarter horses and Thoroughbreds. They ate hamburgers and Frito pie. She never had that same feeling when she and Darren came up here together. It always just seemed like she was fulfilling a duty.

Carolina looked around for the sight of something familiar from her childhood. The new barns for the horses were to the north. Metal buildings, built to withstand the fires that had leveled the old wooden stalls that burned in the awful conflagration in the summer of her sixteenth year. Twenty-three horses killed in the fire or put down. She shivered at the thought.

The smell of food and beer began to fill the air under the metal roof of the stands. Whiffs of perfume and sweat. As she passed by the people standing at the rail and sitting

on the benches, she could hear snippets of familiar conversations like she'd heard when she came up here with her dad. Same conversations, different people.

"What do you think of number nine in the sixth, Phil?"

"Number three is due for a win."

"...and I told Don that I was through with his crap and I wasn't..."

"Number four in the first looks good, don't you think, honey?"

"If it suits you, Babe, here's some money. Get me a beer while you're at it."

Climbing the bleachers, she reached the top row and scanned the crowd of people gathered at the rails of the track. She knew from experience that Darren would be down there, close to the paddock, studying the horses. He was curious, talkative, always in the thick of things. He loved the excitement, the crowds, the high he got from cheering on a horse that he had covered with a wager. *Funny how those things used to seem so charming to me.*

She knew it would be a surprise when he spotted her. Their marriage had been drifting in a sea of indifference, occasionally moored to a charade of interest. An old-fashioned sense of duty had driven her to give up her solitude of this day and make the two-hour drive to Ruidoso to "watch the ponies run." She'd done it to share that with him. He was unaware that she knew he had taken this day off from work, starting the weekend early.

Carolina stood easily, not having to strain over the crowd as a shorter woman would have done. She was comfortable with her size; a strong, tall, broad-shouldered woman, capable, singular. She let her eyes drift over the crowd, the way her dad had taught her years ago. "Look from the farthest to the near," he told her. "Note movement, color, anything different. It's the easiest way to find a cow, a horse, anything or anyone."

She spotted Darren, standing with a new silver belly Stetson tipped to block the afternoon sun. She watched as he talked and gestured, studying the horses entering the paddock. Carolina knew that she should not resent his sense of freedom. She had made choices in her life which had brought her to this turning point with him, while he had gone blithely along, doing whatever suited him.

A petite redhead, hanging on his every word, leaned against Darren, caught up in his enthusiasm. A pile of red hair tied loosely at her neck with teasing tendrils of curls framing her face. Even from where she stood, Carolina could see the heavily made-up eyes laughing into Darren's. Carolina's heart clenched with the realization that he had not come up here alone. She knew. Maybe she had known for a long time. Still, it hurt. She took a ragged breath, trying to hold a coherent thought. *The sorry SOB! How long? Who? Damn him to hell and back!* The humiliation of his betrayal raced with her anger.

Carolina started down the steps, anger welling up and catching in her throat, unsure of what she would do when she reached the bottom. Tripping, she caught herself, annoyed at the outward manifestation of her inner turmoil. How she disliked women who made scenes. Women who couldn't stay "gathered up" as her Daddy used to say. Tears slipped down her face. *I'll be damned if he is going to see me like this!* Knowing that she would chhave until Sunday evening to figure this all out, she headed for the parking lot.

Angrily wiping away the evidence of her pain, she strode quickly to the pickup, fumbling for her keys. The trip back to Roswell seemed so long. There were few people on the road this afternoon. She knew that by six o'clock the traffic would be heavy and unsafe with the Texans who always seemed to be in such a hurry. The road hugged the silhouette of the mountains. There was nowhere to go except straight up or straight down. The curves remained, even after the road had been widened to accommodate the people escaping the heat of the plains, escaping their everyday routines.

She looked down the hill as she drove and noted that many of the old adobe casas had been leveled and replaced by the new homes of the gentlemen ranchers and horse breeders. Rows of trees lined the long drives which carved away the apple orchards of her memory. The familiar pastures were empty of everything except an occasional horse. *What a waste of good grass! What a waste of my life!* She thought as she brought herself back to her immediate problem.

Some way they, or she at least, had thought that they had time to work out their differences. Work driven as she was, focused on her goals, she had failed to notice the slipping away from each other, the separateness of their lives. In the back of her mind, she had known that they would have to talk about this rift between them. *It just takes so much energy—and time. I have so little of either anymore. Between helping Dad at the ranch and teaching at the college, my life is filled.* She had given notice that she was not going to teach this summer, hoping that she and Darren could go out to her dad's place and find the joy that they had somehow misplaced. She tried to visualize the fishing holes as she had last seen them, knowing full well that every time The River ran full, new holes were carved by the turbulent waters. Each time they let the water down from the dam up north, the banks changed, and it was dangerous to assume that you knew anything at all about The River.

Carolina pulled up to the house and left the pickup in the driveway. She checked the mail at the street mailbox and opened the front door to a darkened room. Traveling through the house, nervous, searching. On edge and dissatisfied, she opened the refrigerator and quickly shut it. Carolina filled the teapot and found a tea bag and cup. Once the whistle started on the kettle, she poured hot water over the bag and carried the cup to her favorite chair. The thoughts churning in her mind would not settle. There seemed to be a cloud in her head as she attempted to sort her thoughts from her feelings, her principles from her duty. *What to do?* After sitting there and letting the tea get cold, she *did the only thing that made sense to her.* Carolina picked up the phone and dialed. No answer. *Of course not. It isn't dark yet. Dad considers it a sin to waste daylight. I'll call him later.*

Carolina paced around, nervous, anxious, angry. She pulled down her overnight bag. She stuffed clothes and toiletries inside and looked around to see if she needed anything else. She noticed the stack of tests and, remembering that the final grades would have to go out on Monday, gathered up the pile of papers and her grade log, putting them in her briefcase. *Something else that would have to be done this weekend.*

"Morgan here."

She heard her dad answer and immediately felt better. The sound of his strong, warm voice always felt like a hug.

"Hi Dad, it's me."

"Well, hello Carolina. How are things?"

"Everything's okay. I was thinking about coming out tonight."

"Is everything all right?"

"Mostly. We can talk later."

"Glad to have you, Sugar."

She smiled at that. "Do you need anything?"

"You might bring some coffee; I'm getting a little low."

"Okay. See you soon."

"Drive safe," he cautioned.

"Well! That spoils my plans!" she said, teasing him with the old joke that they used with each other.

"See you soon, girl." The line went dead.

Grabbing her laptop and bag, she turned off the lights on her way out the door.

The long drive to the ranch gave her time to think. If only she could sort out the things that kept running through her mind. *If this was the first time that I had seen Darren with another woman it might be more tolerable. It wasn't. He always just denies my accusation until I begin to think that I'm imagining things. He can charm the rattles off a rattlesnake.* The further she drove, the more the anger welled inside of her, tasting like hot metal on her tongue.

Whoa girl she thought, checking herself. *Back it up and start over. Let's try to keep a steady mind until we can sort this all out.* She knew they had reached an impasse in their marriage. She turned on the radio, hoping to elevate her mood. The mournful country song stirred up memories. The plaintive tone and the lonely words tore at her, reminding her of her first love, Travis. All the years of growing up on neighboring ranches, school dances, the rodeos. Memories of so many years, good years, until they had one day realized that they were in love.

That won't do! She quickly changed the station, searching for something to take her mind off of the mess her life had become. Changing to an old-time rock and roll station raised her mood.

The lights from the house at last. As Carolina pulled into the graveled drive, the old black dog rose and started barking. She stepped out of the pickup and the dog charged her.

"Jake! It's me!" she yelled.

Jake immediately dropped his head in contrition, came forward and began to lick her hand and sniff her.

Morgan came to the door, saw that it was her, and came down the steps smiling. He wrapped her in a bear hug. She relaxed against him and he held her. Carolina leaned back so she could look up into his face.

"Jake charged me. He didn't recognize the truck or me."

"He doesn't hear or see as well as he used to. He's getting old, like me. I should

probably get him a pup to train so he can retire from ranch security."

She nodded at the old joke and he helped bring her things into the house. Morgan noticed her looking at the thin film of dust on the dresser.

"Don't write in it," he said poking her in the ribs.

She responded, "And if I do, don't date it, right?"

"Right."

After dusting the furniture and settling into the familiar room she went to find her dad. He watched her walking down the hallway.

"Carolina, I need to check the wheels tomorrow. See you in the morning."

She retired to her room, disappointed that he didn't want to talk for a while. As Carolina got ready for bed, she studied an old photograph of her mom and dad in a wooden frame on the dresser. It called to mind something that her mother had said not long before she died. "He is ours, Carolina. He loves us but there is a part of his heart locked up some place. He won't talk about it. Maybe someday he'll tell you. But never doubt that he loves us. More than he loves himself. He is a good and honorable man."

Carolina puzzled over these words. They were cryptic and final. It was hard to sleep. Her cell phone rang, and she looked to see who was calling so late. She saw that it was Darren and took a deep breath, bracing herself for the inevitable.

"Were you sleeping?"

"No."

"Where are you?"

"At the ranch."

"Is something wrong?"

"No. I'm going to stay out here for the weekend."

She sensed the pause before he cautiously asked, "Why?"

"I was at the track today."

"Oh? I didn't see you."

"Of course, you didn't. I don't want to talk now."

"Love you, Babe." She hung up without answering.

So much said and avoided. Again. She lay awake for hours, perplexed over what her mother had said and not said and the decisions she had to make about her future.

Chapter 2
The River Incident
1866

Several months after hiring on with the Rocking R, Morgan had been riding near The River, looking for strays, when he came across the man in the water. The terrified stranger was yelling, frantically kicking, trying to remove the boot and spur that were tangled in the belly strap of the saddle on his horse. The horse lunged and pawed, struggling in the cold, churning water. Morgan dismounted and pulled a hunting knife from his saddlebag. Calling above the screams of the panicked horse for the man to remain calm, he eased into the swirling water, the round eyes of the terrified horse staring at him. The man, pleading with Morgan to help him as he gripped the saddle horn, tried to stay aboard the flailing mount.

Morgan moved to the down-river side of the horse where the water didn't pull so hard on him. He struggled to keep from being washed away as he situated himself and felt for the man's leg, pushing it out of the way to reach the belly strap. A solid blow from flailing hooves sent a shock of pain through him. The cold water soon numbed him, and he struggled to hold on to the knife in his stiff fingers. Avoiding the striking hooves, he managed to cut the man from his drowning horse. The frightened stranger grabbed at Morgan, pulling him below the surface of the muddy River. The horse, relieved of his rider and saddle, rolled onto his side and fought to right himself as he floated with the rapid current. Morgan watched the panicked horse until he was out of sight.

The two men clawed at the moving water, striving to stay afloat.

"Don't stop," Morgan yelled at the man. "Keep moving, slow."

Gasping for air, they were pushed downstream before they both managed to reach the other side and pull themselves onto the bank. The man, weak and coughing, raised his hand in gratitude. Morgan, choking, his head spinning, lost in the crushing feeling as electrical currents coursed through his body, could not respond.

The hairpin curve in The River was turbulent that day from the spring runoff, the waters receding but still moving swiftly. The red sand, rolling like ball bearings, pulling things under, deep into the unforgiving River. That fateful incident had brought him forward to another time and place.

Chapter 3
Glorieta Pass
1862

The pain tore grunts from Morgan in ragged breaths. Each jolt of the wagon ripped an unintended cry from the stalwart man. He raises his head and, unable to see over the side of the buckboard, lays back, concentrating on making no noise to add to the dismal sounds of an army in retreat. Morgan lay in a pool of blood and wondered if it was his. Next to him a soldier lay writhing, crying, still bleeding from the cauterized stump of what used to be his leg. The blood-soaked bandages drew no flies. Other men pressed against him within the confines of the wagon, moaning and calling out.

The March air was brittle with cold that lay like wet sheets over the wounded men. He tried to be thankful that he was alive. Still, the searing, bone-crushing pain was enough. The flesh and blood that stuck to his clothes was beginning to stiffen. Part of Corporal August. The Corporal was in front of him as they engaged the enemy at Pidgeon Ranch, at the mouth of the Glorieta Pass. The bullet that ripped the hole in the Corporal had slammed into Morgan's leg, buckling him before the onslaught of the Blue Bellies who descended on them.

Morgan closed his eyes against the memory. Moans and cries from the men in the other wagons mixed with the sounds of an army on the move. Orders being given, the crunch of wheels on the rock- strewn road, the creak of saddle leather, the swearing of the men guiding the caissons down the rocky angles; the grunts of other men, less crippled, holding up those who could still travel, stumbling in tattered formation. The litters, carrying the more severely wounded men, dragged behind exhausted horses, scratching tracks which pointed down the Santa Fe Trail.

How long has it been since we engaged Chivington? What have we lost? How long have I been unconscious? God! It hurts!

Morgan stared up, concentrating on the white clouds scudding across the faded sapphire sky. He forced his mind to study the changing shapes, willing himself to think about anything but the battle and the pain. The wet, sickening smell rose from the blood-soaked wooden boards of the wagon.

He thought back to the two days they had bivouacked at the Johnson Ranch and Stage Stop. For those two days she had been there. Sophia. The prettiest girl he had ever seen, with eyes the color of a stormy summer sky.

The supply train had been left under Scurry's guard at the Station along with heavy guns and extra mounts. When they were overrun by Chivington's men the inhabitants of the ranch were overwhelmed by the wounded and dying men who soon poured down upon them after the battle at Glorieta Pass.

The way station didn't have the means to provide for all of the maimed, beaten men who had descended on them after the battle. The troops bivouacked there for two days, resting the horses and men, tending to the wounded and preparing for the retreat south. The two women doctored and cooked for the embattled men.

Morgan's eyes followed the tall, dark headed woman as she moved from one man to the next, caring for each in his turn. He waited impatiently, the nausea seeming to emanate from his wound, crawling up into his throat, choking him.

She finally approached, a tiny smile touching the corners of her mouth. Morgan focused on that mouth, trying not to groan or retch with the pain.

"My name is Sophia. I'll do what I can for you. I'm going to clean the wound first and try to stop the bleeding. A little bleeding is all right because it will purge the wound. I'm glad that no one tried to cauterize it with gunpowder. That stops the blood but leaves an ugly wound to heal."

"I told the medic to leave it and use a tourniquet. I've seen those burned holes."

"That was wise of you. I don't have much for the pain, but I'll get you some willow tea when we're finished. Are you able to talk?"

"Not much," he said, clenching his teeth.

Sophia bathed him and bandaged his wound, wrapping the strips of cloth tightly around his quivering, exposed thigh. Morgan tried to lift his head to look at the wound but fell back, too weak from loss of blood to hold himself upright.

As she bathed and tended to his wound she talked, keeping his attention.

"What's your name, sir?"

"Morgan Donnally."

"My name is Sophia Chatham. My father has a ranch about four days ride from here. I came to visit my friend, Delia. She helped me feed the hands when we worked our cattle, and I came up here to help her do the same."

"It's a good thing for us that you were here. This is a good time of year to gather cattle, since they're weak from the winter forage."

"It was frightening to see Chivington's troops swoop down on us. Everyone scattered for the hills except Delia, her dad and me."

"It was pretty scary from our side, too."

"After they left, you men came straggling in. We don't have much to help you by way of food and medical supplies."

He studied her face as he sipped the willow bark tea that she offered him and then, once she had moved on to the next bed, tasted the bone broth, grateful for her kind ministrations.

Morgan lay awake in the gray light of dawn, listening to the awakening camp. The pain gnawed at his le; the loss of blood made him dizzy each time he tried to rise.

Soon the men were stirring. The doctors and aides filtered in. He watched for Sophia and was relieved when she entered with a small group of women. Mrs. Canby, a Union officer's wife, had set up this hospital and gathered the women who worked under her, caring for all the wounded, North and South, even though the Southern flag flew over the Palace of the Governors.

Morgan looked out of half-closed eyes as the women fanned out and started ministering to the soldiers. He studied her as she slowly worked her way towards him, refusing to meet his eyes. He watched her shoulder blades moving, covered with a blue and white shirtwaist. They looked like angel wings holding her, allowing her to hover over the men. He must have dozed because the next thing he heard was,

"Hello, sir. How are you this morning?"

Morgan did not reply, entranced by her well-formed mouth and the deep, intelligent eyes which searched his face for any sign that he heard her. He lay with one arm over half closed eyes, his mouth drawn down.

She continued to talk to him, sharing the news around town, coaxing him to talk, discussing local news and avoiding the War and the decimation of the troops.

He finally spoke, hesitant at first, anxious that she not leave his side. Morgan searched for something to say which would keep Sophia near him.

"It was a cruel and inglorious two days. Chivington came down off the hills and took our supply train. You must have seen that from the house. Burned everything."

"I saw that. They bayoneted the mules and horses."

"The scouts gathered a few but we are short of enough to take us back to Texas. Eighty-five wagons gone. All of our supplies." He shook his head, ruefully. Her eyes were intense as she studied him, taking in his words.

"I am so sorry to hear this, Sergeant."

He extended his hand to her. "Call me Morgan, ma'am."

"Not in public, sir," she said as she pulled her hand out of reach.

Morgan noted the promise in her words and looked around at the men who were staring at him, scowling at the time and attention he was hoarding.

"I'll be reading later."

"I'll be here."

"Good. Then I won't have to go looking for you."

He smiled weakly at her little flirtation.

After tending to the soldiers' wounds, she passed out plates of stew with a slab of bread on top. Sophia settled herself in a chair not far from Morgan's cot and began reading. The men who could, gathered around, sitting on the bunks of the wounded and on the floor, leaning against the walls or on branches that they used for canes. Morgan turned on his side. He tucked the blanket under his wounded leg and propped his head in his left hand. He studied the indentation at the base of her throat, wondering what it smelled like, how it tasted.

Leaning back, he closed his eyes so he could concentrate on the rise and fall of her voice. The laughter which burst from her was infectious as she paused to share a funny line in her story. It reminded him of the sound of a covey of quail bursting from their bed ground in the mist of early morning, or the waterfall in the far pasture of the old place in Tennessee.

Two days later, a routine had developed, and he waited in anticipation for Sophia to continue her story. She came to a line in the narrative which caused the room to erupt in laughter and she turned to see if Morgan joined the mirth. He smiled, but he had been daydreaming about her and so missed joining in her delight.

The next morning, he could hear the women laughing and sharing a line from the story.

"Why Madam, it would tickle my liver if you would tell me where you got those clothes."

"Well certainly dear friend, I would be happy to tell you."

The laughter faded away as the women entered the barracks and met the eyes of the wounded.

A week had passed in Santa Fe when the orders to prepare for departure came down. What was left of the Regiment was commanded to assemble before the Palace of the Governors. The Alcalde, whose home Brigadier General Sibley occupied during the battle—claiming to be ill—spoke of the bravery of the men. The merchant brothers Raphael and Manuel Armijo expressed deep regret at the departure of so many good men. Sibley gave the farewell address, thanking the many people who had cared for the wounded and billeted the soldiers during their brief time of occupation. The only sounds were the fractious horses fidgeting and pawing the ground in the frosty morning air.

While Sibley spoke, Morgan sat rigid in the bed of the wagon, crammed hip to hip with other wounded men. He searched the crowd for Sophia. He spotted her, standing shoulder to shoulder with the other women of Mrs. Canby's "Angels of Santa Fe." She raised a gloved hand to shield her eyes from the early morning sun. He smiled when he realized that her eyes were riveted on him. He waved and tipped his hat, wishing that he could swallow the cloud of breath that escaped her lips in the frigid morning air. They had not been permitted a private goodbye. Her dark hair glinted with a fiery red halo as the sun bathed her in the gold dust of morning light.

Jean-Baptiste Lamy, the first Archbishop assigned to Santa Fe, prayed for the safe travel of the troops and the parade of men and wagons began moving through town. Morgan studied the adobe buildings and one-story mud homes. The smell of burning pinon curled from the chimney pipes. Nondescript, bronze-skinned Indians wrapped in ragged blankets stood motionless, eyeing the cavalcade with blank stares. Oxcarts, piled with goods, pulled by shaggy donkeys, plodded down the street. Shawled women, with children gathered in their skirts, waved and blew kisses to their favorites, who silently watched Santa Fe disappear as they headed toward Mesilla in Arizona Territory. Skirting the foothills of the Sangre De Cristos Mountains, hunters scoured for game as the tattered colony veered off from the Rio Grande. It was a rag tag company that retreated down the dusty trail. The rock-strewn road further wore out the starved animals as they struggled to draw the wagons and men back to Fort Bliss. The column strung out for miles; the road scattered with dead or dying animals and abandoned equipment.

Colter stood at the entrance of the tent they shared, studying Morgan as he lay on his bed.

"I heard that you started working the horses. It's about time, old man."

"Six weeks of malingering was all I could stand," Morgan replied.

"I'm glad to see that your leg's healing. I saw some colts necked up to mules. You plan on making teams out of them?"

Morgan grinned. "Not exactly. An old timer taught me that the easiest way to break a colt is to let an old mule do the work. It only takes about two days for those mules to educate them."

"Sounds pretty clever."

"It saves me a lot of work. Those shave tails are always a long day's exercise. Green and unpredictable. Doing it that way leaves me time to work on the bunch that those scouts brought in."

"Here are some old papers if you want to read them. Looks like those Copperheads up north are not happy with the invasion."

"I'm one of them, Colter. I would like to look at those papers," Morgan said.

Colter handed Morgan the stack of old newspapers. "The Lieutenant wants us to join the scouting and hunting expeditions. There hardly seems to be any game being brought in. The soup is getting pretty thin. First light tomorrow. We better turn in early."

"I want to write a letter first."

———◉———

Sophia Chatham
Fort Marcy
Santa Fe, New Mexico

Dear Miss Sophia Chatham,

I hope this missive finds you well. I am sending my best regards from the Regiment to you and Mrs. Canby's ladies. We are forever in your debt for your kind ministrations. It took us many weeks to reach Fort Bliss. We could only make fourteen miles a day with such short rations and our worn-out mules and horses. We skirted the San Mateo Mountains and crossed the Journado Del Muerto in order to evade the Federalists and Indians. They harassed us much. We were ordered to put on as many clothes as we could and take seven days of rations. We were then ordered to burn everything else to prevent their use by those deviling us. We butchered the fallen horses and mules but there was very little to sustain us. The sweet smell of the horses' blood would have sickened me more if I was not so hungry. I fear I have lost my sense of smell. We are in need of much care and rest from our journey. Since there are no supplies for us, men are sent on hunting forays and ordered to appropriate any mules and horses we find. It is now May and we have been here at Fort Bliss for almost two months. The land is poor. I am able to ride but the leg gives me the devil at days' end.—

———⬤———

"Please don't take my horses. How can I make it?" the man pleaded as the soldiers roped and lead the animals from the stand of trees where they had hidden.

"We need them for the War. I'm very sorry. I'll give you a receipt. You can collect from President Davis after this unpleasantness is over. The address for petition is on the paper," replied Colter as he handed the lead lines to a nearby soldier.

Morgan rode close to Colter and leaned down. Speaking softly, he said,

"Colter, why don't we leave him one horse. We might win a convert to our Cause if we don't leave him afoot. It's pretty hard to survive out here without transportation."

Colter looked long into the eyes of his friend, weighing their orders against the wisdom of Morgan's words.

"Turn that bay into the corral, private," he ordered.

Without looking back, he ordered the men to follow him with the rest of the horses that had been gathered on this raid.

As they rode side by side, Morgan said, "Why don't you take those horses back to the garrison and I'll take two pack mules and one man to continue hunting? Or you can go with me and let the soldiers take them back."

"You men, head back with the horses. If you see any game on the way, take it in. Sergeant Donnally and I are going to continue to hunt. Forage along the stream for anything you can find but don't linger. Also, don't overeat. you'll make yourselves sick."

Returning a salute from the men, Colter turned and gathered the lead lines of two pack mules and rode alongside Morgan.

"Good work, Colter."

"Not from the Army's point of view. We were ordered to gather all riding stock. We could be court martialed or worse for what we just did."

"Don't worry about it. As the one in charge of the livestock I can testify that the horse you left was not suitable for our purposes. It looked to me like he had the scours. No telling why he was sick."

"He did look a little peaked," Colter replied, conspiratorially.

"We don't want to pass that along to the men or the other horses. As long as we bring back two packs full of meat, I doubt that anyone will say anything. Let's just be sure that the general gets a big deer steak."

Two days of searching the banks of the stream and the ravines produced two large bucks that were field dressed and tied to the pack saddles of the mules. The men lit a fire and carved two chunks of meat from the deer. With the meat laid on two flat rocks in the middle of the fire, the two friends sat back and watched the flames.

"Should we feel bad about this, Morgan?"

"I don't see why. We've been out here now for three days. One with the men and two by ourselves. We have another day to get back. Do you have anything besides hard tack in your saddle bags?"

"Well, when you put it that way, I guess we do deserve these steaks. It just seems a little greedy to fill our bellies when we're hardly bringing back enough for our men to fill theirs."

"When we take these back, we can head out and try to do this again, without the troops for gathering mounts. We'll cover more ground that way."

"We may be a little soft for this job, my friend."

"I am, for truth. I can't stand taking from people who have to work so hard to scrape by. I know what it's like to have everything taken from you."

"I forgot about that, Morgan. The Jayhawkers in Tennessee. At least we're doing it for the Cause. Well, I think these steaks are done. Let's let them cool a while and I'll cover the fire."

Colter and Morgan returned to base and were greeted by the men with cheers when they saw the loaded pack mules.

Reporting to the commander, Morgan said, "Sir, we are returned from the hunting foray. We brought back some deer and quail. No enemies. We collected twelve horses and five mules. My men were sent back three days ago with the mounts. Sergeant Colter and I went on and found some provisions. I have ordered a venison steak prepared for you tonight."

A smile crossed the general's face.

"Thank you, Sergeant. Dismissed."

Morgan returned to his bunk and pulled out the letter that he had begun several days before.

——●——

—A few days break in this missive due to excursions. I am now back at camp with time to add to this letter. I dread the long road to San Antonio. No doubt we will start back the way we came and so only a small detachment at a time will start out. This is so that the watering holes will have time to recharge before the next detachment. It will also give us time to remount the Brigade. Of the thirty-two hundred troops who went North, about five hundred were captured and we lost another five hundred to combat and disease. We are at present seeking supplies and remounts to continue our journey to San Antonio. I wish fervently to continue our correspondence and wish to tell you a little of myself by way of introduction. As I mentioned to you at Fort Marcy, I am from Tennessee. My parents had a place in Franklin where we had a horse farm. I was an only child due to the scarlet fever which took my older sister and my parents perished in the fire set by the Jayhawkers. We were burned out. I traveled to Texas, looking for work. When President Davis put out a pronouncement of conscription, I joined the Second Texas Mounted Rifles. I would much rather ride than walk and since I owned a horse and rifle, it was a good fit. It also kept my belt buckle from rubbing up against my backbone. It was hard times in Texas. Still is. No one needed day workers. There was no coffee, meat, shoes, medicine, or clothes to shelter or keep body and soul united. The country was in desperate want. Brigadier General Sibley gathered three regiments of mounted Texans and we rode north. Mesilla, the new seat of the Territory of Arizona, had recently been taken by a company under Major Isaac Lynde and was being held by the Unionists. Our orders were to take back Mesilla, then Santa Fe, and move on to the gold fields of Colorado, after taking Fort Union. The gold in those fields would have given a necessary infusion to the Southern Confederation. That we failed to do so I believe is due in large part to our leadership. A General whom I will not name appears to have been in the rear guard and in his cups. Chasing gold seemed at the time like a grand adventure. If we had taken those gold fields and moved on to California and kept the new territory out of the hands of the Federalists we would have fulfilled our mission. If we had secured California and opened the seaports for Southern commerce, it might have changed the direction of this war and helped to end it sooner. We were headed towards those gold fields of Colorado on that fateful day when I met you under the most inauspicious circumstances. I would not change that now for anything. I found a true treasure that day. I pray our friendship continues.

I am most Respectfully Yours,
Morgan Donnally,
Second Texas Mounted Rifles
Fort Bliss, Texas CSA

Chapter 4
At the Ranch
May 2012

Carolina awoke slowly, reluctantly. She kept her eyes closed as she inhaled the familiar morning scents. Gradually, she opened her eyes. The hollow, reedy voice of the announcer was talking about the weather. *Dad must be listening to the old Bakelite radio on the refrigerator. Something to fill the silence.*

As a child, she would wake to the sound of her mom and dad talking softly in the kitchen. *I miss Mom. At least what I remember.* Carolina knew that her dad did, too, but they didn't talk about it. She also knew that the first thing he did in the morning was to look at the sky and smell the air, checking the weather. Facing toward The River.

She rolled herself out of bed and caught the smell of breakfast. As the familiar scent of biscuits and fried beef wrapped itself around her, her mood lightened. She smiled. Her dad didn't eat pork. He called it farmer food. He ate beef. His own. She visualized him, moving a piece of tallow around the pan, greasing it, then slicing thin strips of beef and watching it sizzle in the old cast iron skillet. It made her hungry.

Darren never ate breakfast at home. She had gotten used to eating a piece of toast over the sink and washing it down with a cup of coffee. *Darren likes to eat from the burrito truck that comes around the shop each morning. No wonder he's gaining weight. I can't say anything, my pants are getting a little snug, too.*

Morgan heard her stirring around and called down the hall.

"How many eggs, Carolina?"

"Just one, Dad," she called back, wrapping herself in a robe as she hurried to the kitchen.

She poured a cup of strong, black coffee and sat down at the corner of the old wooden kitchen table. Her dad had put a new top on that table long ago.

It was worn now from all the years of meals, homework, bread making and the cleaning of his guns. A table of memories.

"Good morning, Sunshine. How'd you sleep?"

"I slept fine, Dad," she said, trying to match his morning greeting. It fell short.

He turned to look at her but said nothing. Setting a plate in front of her, he reached around her and placed his own at the end of the table. After refilling their cups, he sat at the end of the table in his favorite spot.

Morgan pushed the platter of biscuits toward her. "I better not Dad. I'm putting on weight."

He smiled tenderly at her and said, "You come from a long line of easy keepers. Some men like that."

He always knows the right thing to say.

"This looks great, Dad," she said, poking at the orange yolk of her egg.

Morgan watched her and volunteered, "Arlene brings them to me."

"Oh? Is she still single?"

"Yes," he said briefly, cutting off any more conversation on the matter.

They sat in comfortable silence as they finished their meal. He lifted the chair, careful not to scrape the floor, and placed it quietly under the table. She had never known him to scrape a chair—or slam a door for that matter. He was a quiet, precise man, an old-fashioned gentleman. She missed that. There was a grace about him. A quiet dignity. An economy of motion that she had never seen in another man.

"I have to check the waters; do you want to come along?"

"Yes. Let me get dressed."

"I thought you already were."

It was a gentle reminder to come to the table dressed and ready to work. She had gotten into the habit of not dressing before she had her coffee. City style.

"I'll hurry."

"I'll be in the truck."

Carolina dressed quickly and pulled her hair into a ponytail. As she hopped into the old ranch pickup she noticed the headlights shining on a new Dodge dually.

"When did you get that, Dad?"

"Two weeks ago."

She knew his habit of trading up and using the last "new" pickup for ranch work. He didn't believe in spending time repairing vehicles if he could avoid it. He always said that there were more important things to do with his time. That was just one way that he was able to keep from hiring much help. He had passed on his thrifty ways to her. It was just another thing that she and Darren did not have in common. He always wanted the newest and best of everything. She had given up arguing about that. She put as much as she could into her retirement account and kept her mouth shut.

She started when she heard Travis's name.

"...and a couple of other fellas got together and went to the dealership to buy new trucks. Sometimes you get a better deal when you buy in bulk." He ended in a chuckle, amused at his own joke.

"What did you do with the last one?"

"I gave it to Doroteo. He dropped the transmission in his."

Frugal and generous. That's my dad. Sometimes quoting Scripture about having

something to give to someone in need.

"Doroteo brings Maria's tamales by whenever she makes them. It's a good trade."

"Sounds like it. I miss her tamales."

It was getting light by the time they reached the first water tank. He climbed up to see if it was full and climbed back down. Carolina stepped out of the pickup and stood watching the sunrise. Startled by a second person in the truck, the cows began to stir. She watched as the cattle rose, hips first, in unison and moved away from their bed ground. Morgan pulled the loop that kept the windmill pumping, letting it swing free. The pump shaft quit its slow up and down motion. She was always amazed at how little wind it took to keep those blades turning. Carolina stood still, recalling her childhood. "Remember when I used to ride the pump shaft up and down when you checked the waters?"

"I do," he said. "We can come back when the wind's blowing more if you want to do that."

"No thanks, Dad. Only in my memories."

As they drove up to the next pasture gate, her dad stepped out of the pickup, remarking, "Someone has put a witch's tit in the wire. I'll just be a minute."

Reaching for the fence pliers in the door of the pickup, he leaned over the truck bed, snipped off a piece of baling wire and walked to the gate. She watched as he cut off the twisted wire and tossed it into the bed of the truck. He formed a small loop on the end of each loose wire and threaded a new piece of wire through each loop. He then leaned back and pulled the wire tight, finishing the repair.

Morgan stepped to the fence post and pulled the wire loop off the gate post. Dragging the gate out of the way, he motioned for her to drive through. Carolina scooted to the driver's side and drove the truck far enough for her dad to latch the gate behind them. He returned to the pickup. Dropping the pliers in the pocket of the door he said,

"I appreciate that someone is trying to help but it's just as easy to do it right. If you don't have time to do it right, when will you have time to do it over?"

THAT motto is burned into my brain. "Dad, I'm sorry I couldn't stay long enough to help you finish putting in all of those sealed units. Do we need to do that this weekend?"

"No. We're almost finished with ours. Next week we work on Travis's. Now, instead of greasing the gears so often, we shouldn't have to do it but once a year. It'll save us both a lot of time and wear and tear on the knees from going up and down the windmills."

"It's good that everyone still believes in neighboring. He's a good man. How are his girls?"

"Callie is at the head of her class. Carly rides with him most of the time. She prefers a horse but will ride in the pickup if she has to. She's a pistol. Do you want me to have him and the girls over while you're here?"

"No, Dad. I have papers to grade before Monday. I'm surprised that he lets Carly ride, considering her mom's accident."

Carolina stared out of the window, hoping that her dad didn't notice the change in her voice.

She knew when Travis's wife died, she had gone to the funeral. After all these years, her heart still jumped at the mention of his name. Darren brought that up sometimes when they had a fight. He was jealous of her first love. She should never have told him about Travis. She thought that they were sharing in order to get closer and that she could trust him with her secrets. Now she knew better. He kept his own secrets, from his past and even now.

"Dad, I'm taking the summer off. I'll be out here in a couple of weeks."

"Glad to have you. Can you help string some wire?"

"Wouldn't miss it for the world," she said, and reached to pat him on the knee.

Morgan and Carolina scraped their boots on the worn-out hemp mat that was stretched in front of the door and entered the house. Morgan headed toward his office and asked Carol to fix some sandwiches.

"It's too early for supper, so how about something light for now. I have calls to make and some paperwork to do."

"Sure thing, Dad."

She pulled out the cooked roast and sliced a generous slab for her dad and a thinner slice for herself. Getting the mayonnaise and jalapenos from the refrigerator, she next picked a yellow onion from the bowl on the table and cut thin slices. After assembling the sandwiches, she went outside to get the sun tea from the front yard. Her Dad always started the tea first thing in the morning. Wiping off the dirt from the bottom of the jar, Carolina remembered what he had taught her about not putting any glass jar full of liquid on the wooden porch. It was too easy to start a fire with the refraction of the jar. Especially with clear liquids. *So much that her dad had ingrained in her.*

After serving her dad, Carolina retreated to the kitchen where she set down her plate and glass at her usual place, then went to retrieve her briefcase. She stacked the papers on the table and began to nibble on her sandwich as she perused the tests. Soon she was engrossed in the essays and the afternoon slipped by.

Picking up the phone, Morgan dialed his neighbor. "Tom, this is Morgan. Did you plan on going to the sale Monday? ... Good. How about meeting me around two o'clock at the Rancher's Cafe? We need to talk about something. Did you ever find those yearlings of yours? ... No, I didn't find mine, either. Doroteo is missing one and I think Eldrige has lost a couple. Travis is still looking for one. Doroteo has something that may be of interest to all of us. I'll give the rest of the guys a call later tonight. Goodnight."

Carolina walked into the office and heard the tail end of the conversation.

"What's that all about, Dad?"

"Can't talk about it now. How about some Mexican food? Juana's is open until eight tonight."

"Sounds good."

The distance to Dickson was traveled in companionable silence as they listened to the radio. He rolled up the windows, sealing out the dust that curled into the cab. Morgan's large fingers rolled the edge of the knobs on the radio as he dialed, trying to find the news.

Entering the cafe, Morgan spotted Eldrige and family dining at a back table and approached them. "How are you folks doing?"

Mona and the children greeted him with shy smiles. Morgan turned to Eldrige. Lowering his voice he said, "Eldrige — Tom, Travis and I are going to meet at two on Monday at the Rancher's Cafe. It's about the missing calves. You might want to join us."

"I'll be there."

Carolina and Morgan found an empty table and picked up the menus. Looking around, he waved at those he recognized.

"I'm going to get tamales, Dad."

"No one makes better tamales than Maria, so I guess I'll have some red enchiladas. Sooo, Carolina, tell me about your plans this summer."

"I just need a breather. Darren and I are having trouble. I'm not ready to talk about it."

"Good enough, sweetheart."

On the way back to the ranch, Morgan unbuttoned a shirt pocket and pulled out his cell phone. Punching a number, he soon heard Travis's voice on the other end.

"Travis? Morgan here. I got hold of Tom and Eldrige. We're going to meet at two at Rancher's Cafe on Monday. That good for you? ... Good enough. See you at the Sale Barn."

"Dad, am I on speed dial?" Carolina asked with a twinge of jealousy in her voice.

"Of course! You're number one."

"That makes me feel better. Are you having trouble?"

"Nope. Not yet. I'd just as soon not talk about it."

Jake rose to meet them as they stepped out of the truck. He waited for Morgan to open the door and let him in. Morgan filled the bowl with dry food and put half of a can of dog food on top of that. The black dog wagged his tail in appreciation and stuck his nose in the bowl.

Carolina turned on the TV in the living room and sat down, pulling off her boots and tucking her legs under herself. Morgan sat down in the easy chair but as he flipped through the few channels available on the antenna, he found nothing worth watching and both soon retired to their rooms.

Carolina took a hot shower and lay deep under the patchwork quilts, relaxed and full. A peace was settling over her. She knew that she could no longer live with Darren. She couldn't live with a man she didn't trust. She had made her decision and now she just needed to figure out the logistics. She slept much better that night.

Waking to the smell of strong coffee and frying steak, she dressed quickly and hurried to the kitchen. Pouring a cup of coffee, she said, "Good morning, Dad. How was your night?"

"Right as rain, Sunshine. How many eggs?"

"Two."

After the plate was set in front of her, she reached for the sliced tomatoes and salt.

"Where did these tomatoes come from?"

"Doroteo's hot house. His garden tomatoes won't be ready for another six weeks or so."

"Thank you, Doroteo," she said.

Morgan watched as she broke the orange yoke with yesterday's biscuit and ate in silence. Sensing that now might be the time to talk, he began his attempt to get her attention. He pushed the saltshaker against the side of her plate.

"No thanks, Dad," she said, not looking up.

He said nothing but waited a couple of minutes. He then pushed the pepper shaker against her plate. She looked a little annoyed but said nothing. Next came the jar of jam. Nothing. Finally, he pushed the sugar bowl against her plate, eliciting a small smile as she recognized the game he played to get her to talk when she did not know how to start.

"Do you want to talk about it, Carolina?"

"I guess we should. I saw Darren at the track yesterday. He wasn't alone. This isn't the first time. Every time I ask him about these things, he just denies it and says I'm crazy. He gets me believing that I really am."

"Was she a little redhead?"

"Yes! Did you see him?"

"I did. The week you took the OEA girls to Albuquerque."

"Daa-aad. Why didn't you say something?"

"I tried but you didn't want to hear me. He needed enough rope to hang himself. You don't need to keep dragging this out, Carolina."

"I am going to do something, now. I'm going to file for divorce. I wish I had known for sure before this."

"You've been torn up for a long time, but you had to reach the point where you could do something. Now you can. Travis saw them at the Speedway one Saturday."

"Travis knows?!"

"Sugar, nearly everyone knows. No one wanted to hurt you. Now that you have seen for yourself maybe you can stay gathered up and see this through."

"What about the ranch?"

"I checked with the attorney a few months ago. Everything is in order. No money from the ranch was ever co-mingled with his and the ranch has been in your mom's name and yours since your dad died."

Carolina looked up at him, sharply. "I thought it was in your name after you married Mom."

"No. I was just the guardian of you and the caretaker for the ranch until you were old enough to decide what you wanted to do."

"But I don't know, Dad."

"I know that. You are going to have to make some decisions soon. It's been a long time coming. We'll talk about that later. For now, you need to take care of this Darren thing."

"He'll be home tonight. I'll talk to him then."

"Keep your head. Don't let him sidetrack you, make you feel sorry for him. This isn't the first time, and it won't be the last. You were never suited to pair up."

"It's just a shame that it has taken me nine years to find that out. I better get packed. I want to have time to figure out what I am going to say before he gets home."

Morgan kissed her on top of the head and went out the back door towards the barn. He threw the words over his shoulder, "You'll figure it out."

Carolina reached up and pushed the button on the visor to open the garage door. *Darren isn't home yet. Good!*

She went to the mailbox and gathered Saturday's mail. Opening the door to the empty house, she found little comfort being in the house that she and Darren had purchased together. It seemed cold and unwelcoming to her now.

What to do first? She put on the tea kettle and then changed her mind. Reaching into the cupboard, she pulled down the Crown Royal bottle and got a 7-Up from the refrigerator. Carolina slowly stirred the drink with her finger as she made a plan.

First, she would separate her mail from his, then pack a suitcase for him. *The less time he spends in the house, the less likely he is to get abusive or try to talk me out of the divorce. How should I begin this conversation?* She mulled this over as she finished her drink and poured herself another one.

Carolina finished her tasks and sat in the wing back chair, sipping the drink. Soon nausea overtook her, and she ran to the bathroom. She knew that she was trying to purge all of the bad feelings churning inside. She did NOT want to have this confrontation—she had been putting it off for months and this was why. It made her physically ill to think about confronting Darren and ending their nine-year marriage.

The sound of his pickup in the drive woke her. He opened the door and paused, valise in hand. He turned on the light and said, "Hi, Babe. What are you doin', sittin' in the dark?"

"Waiting for you."

"Oh yeah? What's up?"

"I saw you at the track on Friday."

"Oh?" He paused. "I didn't see you."

"Of course, you didn't. You were with that little redhead again."

"You're crazy! I went up there alone and I came back alone."

"You might have but you were up there with her."

"You're imagining things, Carolina. Who's been putting these ideas in your head, again?"

She did not respond to the familiar accusations.

Sighing, as if in capitulation to her unreasonableness, Darren said, "Paul wants me to buy an allowance horse for him to train. I told him I would get back to him."

"Why didn't you ask me to go with you?"

"You never want to go. You're always busy. Besides, it was just business."

"I know what I saw, Darren."

"Carolina, I'm not going to answer to you about everywhere I go. I don't ask you to tell me everything you do."

"All I do is work."

"I don't know that."

Once again, the circular argument had spun away from her accusations and made her question what she had seen.

"You can deny it all you want, but you and I both know that this is not the first one. I don't even care who she is. You were seen at the Speedway with her and also when I went to Albuquerque."

"I don't know who's been lying to you. Is it that damn Travis? He never has gotten over you. Is that what this is about?"

"You know it isn't about him. I want a divorce."

"I won't have it!" he said, clenching his teeth. "I'll kill you before I let you go."

"That works for me because I would rather be dead than married to you!"

There was stunned silence and a look of shocked surprise on his face. Changing his tone, he said, "I never could bluff you."

"And yet you keep trying. I've already packed you a bag. You can get the rest of your things later. Your mail is on the counter."

"Damn Bitch!" were the last words she heard as he grabbed the suitcase and slammed out of the house.

Well! That turned out better than I thought it would. She threw up again and went to bed.

Chapter 5
San Antonio
August 1862

August 24, 1862
Miss Sophia Chatham
Fort Marcy
Santa Fe, New Mexico

Miss Sophia Chatham,

The Regiment has been dismounted. I believe the rebellion of the troops is the cause but much pressure has been brought upon your friend to get the appropriated animals parade ready. I pray that you do not suffer the shortage of food, clothes and medicine that is our lot. The heat is unrelenting. I imagine you in the cool pines around Santa Fe. It gives me comfort. My fervent hope is that you are safe. We are now arrived in San Antonio. It is late August and we are finally back where we started, after two months at Fort Bliss. There have been some desertions. Some men have said that they feel that they do not have a dog in this fight and many say that they are no longer willing to fight for the Cause. I raised my hand in a solemn pledge to defend these States against invasion and subjugation, but I tell you that I understand fully the heart of those who have deserted and gone to their homes or to Mexico. My vow is all that holds me here. Wishing dearly to hear from you.

I am your devoted servant,
Sergeant Morgan Donnally

Second Texas Cavalry Regiment
San Antonio, Texas CSA

———◦———

The unrelenting Texas heat pierced his eyes and penetrated to his brain, leaving him stupefied. He had spent the day saddle-bound, working the horses which had been confiscated from the surrounding area. He stood now, dipping his hand in the bucket, throwing water on his face and neck while he watched the troops in the compound.

Colter appeared beside him. "Haven't you had enough of this heat? Why are you gandering the men. You look like hell. Why don't you clean up and rest before the supper bell?"

"I believe I will," Morgan replied, stunned into the present.

"A wagon unloaded at Headquarters. I think I saw a mail bag."

Setting his bucket down, Morgan called over his shoulder to Colter as he hurried to the wagon, "I sure do hope there's something for me."

"Me too."

———◦———

September 29, 1862
Sergeant Morgan Donnally
Second Texas Mounted Rifles
Galveston, Texas CSA

Sergeant Donnally,

I was most surprised and gratified to hear from you. We were disheartened when your Regiment left. It was much too quiet. The girls expressed sadness at your troop's departure. I am very pleased that your Regiment has returned to your home base. It did lighten our work load a small amount although we never thought it a burden. The Pike Peakers, who defeated you, spent a week drinking and bragging in a most ungentlemanly fashion about their triumph. I wish to go home soon but am delayed for many reasons. My father thinks that I am safer here, surrounded by military men. I do not desire their attentions but am required to attend teas and dances when invited. It does add some gaiety to this dreary existence. I remember when you were here that it was bitter cold, and we could not keep your men comfortable. By the time this reaches you it will no doubt be warm. Put a wet sponge under your hat to keep cool. Also be sure to remind your men to perform their ablutions and masticate well. I remember that was a problem for some of them when they were here. For good health sip cold water as slowly as hot. I welcome correspondence from you and wish to be informed of your recovery and the tasks in which you are engaged. I have received letters from some men in your troop and have passed them on to other ladies; even some who have not ministered to the men. I hope the correspondence lifts their spirits. With my regards,

Sophia Chatham
Fort Marcy
Santa Fe, New Mexico

⇒◉⇐

"Come on, Sergeant, why don't you share your letter with us? Some of us don't get nothin'. We need a little encouragement."

Morgan scanned the letter, making sure that there was nothing he could not share and handed it to the nearest soldier.

"I better get this back in one piece," he warned.

⇒◉⇐

November 2, 1862
Sophia Chatham
Fort Marcy
Santa Fe, New Mexico

Miss Sophia Chatham,

We are removed to Galveston and resolve to hold it for President Davis. It sours me that Texas joined the Union in 1845 and now here it is 1862 and we are fighting to get out. We have battled the Union gunboats and cleared the harbor. We have salt here. In fact, we have plenty of supplies. The ships bring in munitions and food such as we have not seen in many months. We have dried apples, apricots, Eagle Brand Milk and potatoes. We have cans of tomatoes, sardines, pork and beans. We are eating like kings for now. There are fish here. I am not used to sea fish but they are satisfactory. I find that it does not take as much salt to flavor things, having got used to doing without. We go on forced marches to fill our time and keep us ready for the fight. The men have taken to singing a song about eating goober peas as they march along. It is a silly song but keeps up their spirits. Speaking of spirits—Johnny Barley Corn is flowing freely here. That and card games keep the men occupied. Colonel Greene has taken authority over the Regiments. Word has come down that we are to march to Louisiana. Oh, how I wish this war was over. I wish we could walk along this ocean and watch the seagulls. They pick up the mussels along the beach, fly high then drop them onto the rocks below, breaking them open. I must have found a favorite dining place because the shoal is littered with broken shells. I wish I could show this to you. You are in my thoughts and prayers.

I am,
Your Devoted Servant
Sergeant Morgan Donnally
Second Texas Cavalry Regiment
Galveston, Texas CSA

⸺⚬⸺

She had said that she planned to stay in the cooler elevation until fall to escape the heat of the plains. Maybe she returned to the ranch along The River from Dickson. He hoped desperately that his missives had followed her if she had removed to the ranch. Each time there was a call for mail, Morgan posted a letter to Sophia, not knowing whether she received them.

One day, in a fine drizzle of warm rain, he heard his name, "Donnally, Morgan." He hurriedly made his way forward to receive the delivery and sheltered the letter inside his shirt until he found a quiet place on his bedding and opened the missive. A small cluster of dried flowers fell into his hand. He lifted them to his face and inhaled the faint scent, envisioning her. Unwrapping the enclosed paper, he was startled to see a picture. He studied the photograph, rubbing his finger around the edges of the paper card.

———◉———

January 14, 1863
Sergeant Donnally
Second Texas Cavalry Regiment
Galveston, Texas CSA

Dear Morgan Donnally,

I hope you are well. How terrible that you are dismounted. I hope that you soon find enough horses. We are still tending to the results of the battles. One thing I must tell you. I went to a church service and was most surprised to find Major Chivington seated on the dais. D—Yank. He is a Methodist preacher when he is not doing battle with our boys. He stands six-and one-half feet tall and must weigh two hundred and fifty pounds. An impressive man to be sure. He kept his pistol on the pulpit the entire time. I was so amazed at this display that I cannot tell you what message he gave. I had occasion to meet Mr. Loving. He is a cattleman from Texas and has been incarcerated for his Southern sympathies. He had gone up the Arkansas River to Denver and was captured. We were allowed to go to the brig and care for the sick there. I may soon return home. I hope I am not being forward in sending you this photo. There was a traveling photographer in town and I took that opportunity to have one made for you and for my father. The blouse that you see is a new style. It is called a Garibaldi. A seamstress in town has some new magazines from Godey's with all of the latest fashions. I know that it is a vanity with the War going on, but I have not had anything new since I returned from school. Father said that I should order some new clothes. I have pressed some of the flowers that I held for the picture. I miss my father and the ranch. He says I must stay here until after the hostilities are over. He thinks I am safer here. I disagree. My friends and I do enjoy the dances and the buggy rides when we are allowed to go out of the fort to gather herbs and flowers. There are plays and concerts so our time is filled. I would like to share these things with you.

Wishing you the best, I am Your Friend
Sophia Chatham
Fort Marcy
Santa Fe, New Mexico

Chapter 6
The Commission
January 1863

The adjutant general stood on the bed of a wagon holding a notebook while the officers of the Brigade were called to attention.

"Men, there will be new orders given to you with regard to engaging the invaders on cotton and wheat fields. Our rifles don't carry far enough over the open fields. We are too exposed. You are to wear your field jackets to protect against the cotton. We have very little to doctor the deep scratches that we are seeing in the infirmary. You will be instructed how to care for the wounds yourselves. You would be well served if you use some of your tobacco allowance for insect repellent.

The slouch that the men are cooking will continue. Everyone will continue to receive corn meal and we have fresh water. They can still make hoe cakes. Bacon is short. Forays will be made to hunt for meat and greens. I realize that the men are using brown chicory or peanuts to make coffee. Encourage that. What coffee we have has weevils. I suggest that you use it as is. Boil it well. Instruct your men to use the hardtack to thicken whatever soup they can rustle up. It has worms. That should provide a little nourishment."

A rustle of disapproval ran through the assembled men. He continued over the murmuring,

"We still have sow belly for the time being. Use it sparingly. The sutler has some supplies that the men can purchase. Warn the men about counterfeit money. There is a lot of it floating around.

"Encourage your men to be frugal and spend their spare time searching for their own food. The Colonel wishes that he had better news for you. We continue to fight for the Bonnie Blue. The eastern troops are fully engaged. That is all, men."

The officers stood, stunned and confounded, looking at each other.

"Still no shoes or clothes. Now our rations are cut and we have to spend our time trying to find food. The men are hungry and disheartened."

"How do we sell that to our men?" came a voice from the crowd.

"Dismissed!"

No answer came and the men disbursed in small clusters.

Morgan returned to his tent. Colter entered and said,

"Did you give your unit notice?"

"I did. Did you?"

"Yep," Colter said, shaking his head.

"We are not very popular right now. I'm going to stay here and read," Morgan volunteered.

"Me too. I got a new book. My sister sent it. *Inez*. It's supposed to be about the Alamo. Don't know if I trust a story about the Alamo, written by a woman."

"You never can tell. Women surprise you sometimes."

"Not often."

———●———

May 13, 1863
Sophia Chatham
Fort Marcy
Santa Fe, NM

My Dear Friend,

I entertain small hope that this letter of mine will find you, but still I pray. Thank you so very much for the photograph. I have wrapped it in leather and oil cloth and carry it inside my shirt. That is as close as I can get to my heart. How beautiful you are. The blouse is lovely. I am glad that there is not the scarcity of fabric that we endure here. Still have no clothes or shoes for the troops. We hunt to boost our meager rations. Our forage hats come in handy when we find wild onions, roots, and such. I sell my tobacco ration for coins. I have little faith in our paper money. There is much counterfeit which devalues our blue backs and the cost of everything goes up almost daily. Soap is ten dollars a bar and a barrel of flour is seventy dollars. We have been in the bayous and wetlands of Louisiana and have now moved to the timber. Most of those in our detachment are from Missouri and Tennessee and are used to moving quietly through the woods. We are accurate and swift and have pushed the blue coats back. Our rifles are true and our knives are keen. General Taylor has court martialed Colonel Sibley and removed him from command. His commission is broken. Sibley has burned his backside and will now have to sit on the blisters. I was part of the Brigade under Colonel Greene which attacked the federal garrison at Brashear. We suffered a few losses but the sick call continues to be full of men crippled and ill. Many are checked by the company doctor and returned to duty. Some of the more seriously wounded are given opium. It makes them cranky and out of sorts and so adds to the misery of the camp. The troops are debilitated and the camp is infected with typhoid, dysentery, measles, mumps and other ills. The croup is doctored with onions. We use what tobacco we have for insect repellent. I am obliged to be in habitual contact with men of every grade. We have a new Captain. The men say that he has tumefaction of the cranium. -in simple terms- a big head. He has little to recommend him except his stripes. Several men have said that if they could buy him for what he is worth and sell him for what he thinks he was worth, they could pay their way out of this man's army. Scant provisions require us to eat squirrels and the roots of sassafras. We have no yeast and so eat something called johnny cakes. The squirrel is greasy and sits heavy in our bellies. How I long for the bread and biscuits and especially the stew prepared by your hands. I have been told that in the towns around that people used to have biscuit parties but now that there is no food, they have starvation parties and serve only water. How I wish this war was over.

As always, I am,
Your Devoted Servant and Friend
Lieutenant Morgan Donnally
Second Texas Calvary Regiment
Pleasant Hill, Louisiana CSA

Morgan lay on his blankets, reading the well-thumbed Les Misérables. Colter entered the tent they shared and asked, "Still not finished with that book?"

"Almost. I'm reading it slow because I don't have another to replace it. I can't find anything to borrow in camp. Not even a Bible."

"I have one by a fellow named Melville if you want to borrow it."

"What's it about?

"It's about a whaling ship and a captain who loses his leg to a whale. The Lieutenant has one named *Aeneid*. He says it's about the early Romans. I think Billie has one about an Indian, Last Mohican or something like that."

"Hmm. I think I'll give that one a try. Thanks, Colter."

"I'm headed over to Billie's tent. He has a game of cards going. Want to come?"

"No thanks. I think I'll finish this."

Morgan finished the book and lay staring at the patterns on the ceiling of the canvas tent.

A voice broke his reverie.

"Excuse me, sir," an orderly said, saluting. "Your presence is requested at headquarters immediately, sir."

Morgan rose and returned the salute, thanking the man. He could hear the strains of The Blue Juniata drifting through the early evening air. As Morgan strode through camp, he contemplated the story of the Indian maiden in her canoe, pining for her brave warrior. He could see the shadows of four men bent over the campaign table. The silhouettes of the men were bathed in the golden light of the lantern as they intently studied the campaign maps.

Approaching the tent flap, he drew himself to attention and said, "Sir, Sergeant Donnally reporting as ordered, sir."

The Brigadier General looked up from the maps spread before him and said,

"Come in, Sergeant." Returning the salute, he said to Morgan, "At ease."

"Sergeant, the first order of business is this. You are receiving a field promotion to First Lieutenant, effective immediately. Congratulations, Lieutenant."

Morgan stood silent, staring at his commanding officer and then at each face in turn. The smiles assured him that it was true. He saluted and it was returned.

"Thank you, sir."

"The next order of business is this. Here is our current position."

The officer gestured to the map. Morgan stepped forward and studied the map, trying to push down the pride he felt in his promotion.

"The Vermilion is red and on the rise. You are to take a strike force and move up the river. All of our troops to the east are fully engaged and the Federalists have sent an invasion force down the river to see if they can get to the coast. If they succeed, they will be behind our troops. The Feds are on double time, moving this way. Your assignment is to get upriver as quickly as possible to meet them and stop them, if possible. Take an Ordnance man, one specializing in explosives, if we have one, and stop those mortar boats. There are pontoons behind them.

The troops will cross as soon as the pontoons are in place. We must stop those gunboats. The more you can sink, the better. Above all else, bedevil them. Block the river. Slow them down. Take men you can trust. Probably Missouri or Tennessee men. They move fast in the trees. Any questions?"

"Yes, sir. How many men?"

"Take two besides the Ordnance man. Dry camps. No fires. Take what you can find in the commissary but keep in mind that the three men are going to be carrying explosives. Take what the Ordnance man requests. You will send one man back with a report after the first reconnaissance, if possible."

The Commander reached out his hand and said, "Be prepared to leave at first light. Here are your orders and commission. Good luck, Lieutenant."

"Yes sir. Thank you, sir."

Morgan stepped forward and shook the commander's hand. He saluted and shook each hand, then turned, ducking under the tent flap. He took several steps before he stopped to take a deep breath. And another. As he walked toward his tent, he fingered the paperwork in his hand. *Damn! Promoted and told to go blow up the enemy. Damn!* He stopped in front of a noisy tent and peered in. Spotting Colter, he called to him and gestured him outside. Colter rose and followed him.

"I hope this is important, you old sinner. I had a winning hand."

"Big news. Let's walk."

As the men strode away from the encampment, Morgan clapped his friend on the shoulder and said,

"I have been commissioned First Lieutenant."

"What? Congratulations, Donnally! Wait! First Lieutenant? Why?"

"Probably because of these."

"What are those?"

"Orders to take a squad and blow up some boats. I need an Ordnance man and two others. Want to play?"

"Absolutely. You probably want Weasel."

"Weasel?"

"Yes, as in Pop goes the Weasel. He is a little touchy but as good as they come."

"All right. Pick out one more. Go get them. Send for Weasel right away. I've never blown up a boat before."

The men grinned at each other and shook hands.

"Congratulations, Lieutenant," Colter said, coming to attention and offering Morgan his first salute.

Morgan returned the salute and watched his friend disappear into the darkness, then began a new letter about his good news.

———⊷◉⊶———

August 17, 1863
Sophia Chatham
Fort Marcy
Santa Fe, New Mexico

Sophia,

Hello my dear friend. Good news. I have been commissioned First Lieutenant. I am sick and weary of this business and hope by my new authority to make a small difference toward the end of this engagement. I am to be sent on a new assignment up the river. I have preparations to make and so have not much time to write. Know this my beautiful friend, that if things do not go well, that with my last breath I spoke your name. The post roads are closed but I hope to find a way to send this letter to you.

Your Devoted Servant
First Lieutenant Morgan Donnally
Second Texas Calvary Regiment
Louisiana Outpost South, CSA

"Good luck, sir," the soldier said, saluting.

"Thank you, private," Morgan replied, returning the salute.

The young man gathered the reins of the horses and tied them to the saddles. He strung a rope through the bridles, looping each one, and mounted. With a last wave at the men, he turned the horses back to the Headquarters. Morgan and the men had ridden as far as they could, now they were on their own.

"Well, men. Here we go. Keep your mouths shut and your eyes open. We don't know where we'll find the boats. Everyone ready?"

The men nodded in silent agreement, adjusted their backpacks, and fell in line behind Morgan. He set a fast pace, covering much ground in a shuffling trot, hiking north along the Vermillion. The eeriness was intensified by the long beards of gray moss hanging over the small troop. As evening approached, the trees looked like old men watching them from the canopy overhead.

"Let's stop for the night. Cold camp." The men nodded and pulled off their packs, rubbing and stretching, stirring blood back into their shoulders.

Speaking low, Morgan said, "Let's eat and settle down. We are a ways from the river but if anyone snores, you get woke up. I'll take first watch. Listen to the frogs. If they stop singing, wake everyone. Make some paste with your tobacco. Rub it on to keep off the bugs. Especially the chiggers. Anyone needs to smoke, chew some elm bark."

The smell of rotting logs and mud filled the night air as the men shook out their mats and blankets. They pulled hard tack and water from their pouches and ate silently while they studied the surroundings before settling in for the night.

The last shift of the night woke Morgan and he stood, orienting himself to the river. He watched the men with their morning ablutions and pulled hard tack from his pack. Pouring water from his canteen into his metal cup, he left a dried biscuit to soak while he went for a short walk through the trees. A quail, startled by his steps, fluttered up in his face, escaping his grasp. Morgan bent and felt in the grass. He picked up nine warm eggs and put them in his forage cap.

"We need these more than you. These are for the Bonnie Blue Flag, little mother."

Finding a spongy place in the ground, he dug down with his hands until the cavity filled with water. He gently laid the eggs in the water, waiting to see which ones might float. Three of them lay on the bottom of the little pool. Two of them stood on end and swayed in the muddy water, four of them floated to the surface. He placed the floaters back in the nest and gathered the rest in his hat.

Returning to camp, he silently handed each man an egg, placing two into Weasel's outstretched hand. He looked up at Morgan, questioning.

"For your nerves, Weasel."

The toothless man grinned and cracked one of the eggs directly into his mouth.

Morgan wrote in his journal while everyone finished eating then rose, clearing his part of the camp of any evidence of his night. "'Couter up, men," he said as he shouldered his pack. The men followed suit and soon they were again pointed north.

They worked their way through the muck and undergrowth, coming upon an abandoned road, made by laying cane on top of the mud. An abandoned cannon blocked their way. Morgan examined it and found that it had been spiked to prevent its use.

By noon, the men were wet through with exertion, and famished. Morgan knew that he was pushing but he kept the men moving around the unpicked cotton fields, over the broken fences and past the houses, primitive and going to ruin. The men stopped for a breather and scouted the abandoned gardens for any leftover vegetables. Anything that may have reseeded itself from last year. A handful of onions and tomatoes, dried on the vine, were welcome additions to their meager meal.

The sun was no longer visible through the trees when Morgan raised his hand to halt. The small troop fell to the ground without a word and searched through their packs for something to eat.

Colter, silent for much of the march, finally asked, "Morgan, how much further? Do you have any idea?"

"Can't tell. Don't know how good the intelligence was that we received. Maybe six or eight hours according to my instructions. I think the men should spend the rest of the day foraging. It will give them something to take their minds off of the mission. And we need the food."

Colter nodded and rose to give the men instructions. Morgan sat on a musty log and pulled out his journal. He wrote, 'The fences are down and we found a cannon about three days in on an abandoned cane road. We are not yet in sight of the enemy but can smell their camp.'

Morgan overheard Henry and Weasel as they started out to forage. Henry said,

"He's a man you can tie to."

"Yep. He's got a deep bottom." Weasel agreed. "I'd follow that man to hell and back."

"Let's hope we don't have to."

Morgan thought to himself *I certainly hope so, men.*

The men returned from foraging. Their caps were filled with onions, morels, greens, and berries.

"Good job, men!" Morgan held out his hat to receive a share of the bounty. Coulter finished with his meal, stood and announced he would take first watch. He picked up his rifle and moved out of site of the camp. The men gathered for a silent game of cards until it was once again time to settle down. They each looked around, anxious now that they were within shooting distance of the enemy.

An uneasy night left the men nervous, jittery. Morgan sent Colter and Henry to scout. They returned late in the day with a report of arms and men. Morgan let the men rest, knowing that they would be up this night. After a late start, he led the men through the trees, following the banks of the river. The large, bearded cypress rose out of the mud, the river was wide and turbid, the air dank and heavy.

Slowing the advance with his hand, he gestured for the men to hunker down and approach. They soon lay side by side, nervously watching the activity in the camp across the river.

"Move back, men," Morgan whispered. They retreated further into the trees and stood, quietly awaiting instructions.

"Everyone, rest here. Weasel, you sleep if you can."

The men settled around Morgan and the sleeping man, staring off into the trees, lost in their own thoughts.

The moon shed a tattered light through the bearded branches of the trees. Morgan put some hardtack in a cup of water and gently laid his hand on Weasel's bony shoulder. The gray, unshaven man opened his eyes slowly, orienting himself. His bleary eyes focused on the face above him.

Morgan held out the cup with a green onion.

"Here you go, Weasel. it's about time."

The gaunt man struggled to a sitting position. He sipped the water and fished with unclean fingers to gather the last bit of the bread in the cup. Morgan watched as the man gummed the onion. *I wonder how old he is. He never mentioned children. Is he married?* Morgan realized that he knew nothing about the man he was sending on this dangerous mission. Weasel finished the onion and went about constructing a float for the nitroglycerin, black powder, and whale oil. He straightened and pulled his red knit cap down over his ears. Breaking open a cartridge, he smeared gunpowder all over his face. The other men followed suit.

"What do you want us to do?" Morgan spoke into his ear.

"Pray for me and cover my back. If I don't get back, mail this," he said, holding out an envelope.

Morgan looked at the wallpaper folded into a greasy square. The address, scratched in pencil was barely legible. He pulled out the journal from his shirt and carefully tucked it between the pages. He nodded and shook the man's hand. The other men stepped forward and reached for the claw-like hand, murmuring words of blessing.

Weasel eased into the darkness. His knit cap blended with the muddy, red water. It was the only thing visible as he slipped silently into the river, dragging the float with the crocks of bomb components tucked safely in branches.

The men stood, wordless, studying the disappearing form, rifles at the ready. Morgan lifted his field glasses, following the dim figure as he moved from boat to boat, patching the explosives to the hulls just about the water line.

They could see the explosions begin before the sound reached them. One after another, two mortar boats and a pontoon moored close behind shattered and filled the air with debris. The thunder of concussions rolled toward the waiting men. The crackle of fires threw burning debris, showering the boats with a filigree of lights. As the mortars exploded, a kaleidoscope of colors filled the air. The deep concussion of the mortars going off continued as the enemy camp came alive with shouts.

Morgan searched the river for his ordnance man, now thick with suspended matter, dead fish, and turtles. He saw parts of a man's body floating slowly with the current. Hoping against hope that it was a Union man, he stepped into the water and studied the parts. A Confederate jacket, ragged, swirled by. An arm, bare and mangled reached upward, as if in supplication. A red knit cap, filled with matter, spun slowly as it slid by. He watched the drift of the river carry away the first casualty of his command.

"Come on, men, let's get out of here," Morgan whispered, loudly.

The men, stunned and frightened, ran ahead of him through the trees. They traveled like that, running and catching their breath then running again, through the night, heading south. Morgan took the lead and changed directions, headed toward a hill of large rocks, climbing upward. The men exchanged glances but followed. He stopped and waited for the men to catch up. When they all gathered around him, chests heaving, he said, "Be careful not to turn over any rocks, don't scratch anything. If we don't leave a trail, they will quit following us and we can change directions and head home."

The ragtag band of brothers entered the encampment seven days later. Tattered and shaking with exhaustion, they were greeted with handshakes and slaps on their thin shoulders. Morgan dismissed his small cadre with salutes and staggered to headquarters. Coming to attention he said in a voice hoarse with exhaustion, "Sir, Lieutenant Donnally reporting, sir."

The Commander wheeled around to look at him and said, "Good God, man! Come in, sit down."

Morgan stepped into the tent and collapsed on a stool.

"Lieutenant, did you accomplish your mission?"

"Yes sir. I lost one man."

"Son, see to your men, retire and report this evening to my tent." He placed his hand on Morgan's shoulder and patted him roughly.

Morgan woke groggily to the sounds of camp. No singing. No instruments. Just murmurings. He stood and looked out of his tent at the dismal sight of men, emaciated, heads hung low, slowly going through the motions of preparing what meager supplies were on hand. Colter still lay asleep on his bed.

Morgan gathered a bucket of water, stripped and washed himself. He found a shirt left behind in his bedding and slipped it on. Exchanging his forage hat for his new Kepi, he examined it, rolling it around in his hands. The gray wool and black leather brim were decorated with one row of gold soutache braid, the band of yellow signifying that he was cavalry. He pinched it into shape and set it on his head, leaving the forage cap on top of his worn-out excursion clothes. After checking on his men, he again headed to camp Headquarters.

"Sir, Lieutenant Donnally reporting, sir."

"Come in, Come in. You can write your report tomorrow, just tell me what happened."

"Well sir, we were about five days in when we found the mortar boats and pontoons. Weasel, my ordnance man, was able to patch explosives to both boats and one pontoon, blowing them up. We effectively blocked the river for transport, sir."

"Good job, good job. What else?"

"I lost my ordnance man. David Jackson Thomas, sir. The men called him Weasel. He asked me to mail this." Morgan held the letter out to the officer. Both men stared at the folded wallpaper, each one holding a corner of the last missive of a soldier to his wife.

"I'll see that it gets posted. Rest, son. We're moving out day after tomorrow."

Morgan saluted and turned to go. He stopped, reaching for the tent flap. He turned slowly to face his commander and said,

"Sir, he did his best, angels could do no more."

The older man nodded; his mouth pulled into a thin, tight line.

Morgan walked back through the camp, looking around at the men kicking dirt on the flames of their cook fires, preparing to sleep. Pulsing fires threw glowing stars of embers upward. He went to his tent and stood there, looking out at the dismal encampment, lost in thought. He continued to stare into the darkness until the glow of campfires faded to smoky bronze orbits.

Morgan received a letter from Sophia and having no paper to respond, turned her letter ninety degrees and in small script wrote over her words, cross hatching the paper.

⸻⬥⸻

September 25, 1864
Sophia Chatham
Fort Marcy
Santa Fe, New Mexico

Dear Sophia,

We have departed Louisiana and returned to Galveston. I may have to learn to swim. Laugh. We are all dauncy. We have had a hard travel back here. Patrolling the coast is not nearly so rigorous as the excursions in Louisiana. I hope never to see that place again. I will always remember this. I saw an old black preacher on a street corner praying for wisdom and peace for our nation. To that I say amen. One thing that we have here in abundance are women that the men call romps. There are no passes to leave camp, but the romps call out until some men go to meet them and others desert. We do not have the extra men to chase after them. My company has been assigned to the Seventh Texas Calvary Brigade. I am short of paper and so have used your letter and turned it sideways. I wish I could save this letter as I have the others, but we do what we must. I hope you can read it. I have only one stamp to send this. How I wish this was all over and I could get back to New Mexico. I wish to speak to you of my future plans. They can only be fulfilled with you. I have much to say to you that can only be said in person.

I am always,
Your Devoted Servant
Lieutenant Morgan Donnally

Seventh Texas Calvary Regiment
Galveston, Texas

Chapter 7
Mustered Out
July 22, 1865

After months of rumors, word finally came down. The War was done. Surrender in Galveston of the Trans-Mississippi operations by General Edmund Kirby Smith was accomplished on June Second, Eighteen and Sixty-five.

Morgan lay on his bunk, emotions cascading through him. Elation, fear, indecision. *Should I go back and see if there's anything left in Tennessee, first? The war's been over for months now. The only I place I can call home is that girl in New Mexico. Would she think I'm not coming back to her if I go to Tennessee first? Better find her first and then sort it all out.* Fear that she might change her mind when she saw him again drove his decision. Suddenly his heart began to pound. He was finally free to get back to New Mexico and the blue-eyed girl who filled his dreams.

Colter entered the barracks and kicked Morgan's bunk.

"It's done, old man. We're going home. I don't know what took so long. Lincoln died April of this year. General Smith surrendered on May 26th in Galveston."

"They may have had to wait until that Cherokee General Stand Watie surrendered. That didn't happen 'til last month. But the surrender has gone through! Great God Almighty, Thank You!" Morgan said, looking heavenward.

"Thank the Lord. Speaking of which—when I die, I hope the Good Lord takes into account the time I spent in this man's army."

"It has been enough hell for an eternity, that's for sure."

"You received the red badge of courage. I'm glad that your leg healed. I'm getting out without a scratch. Where are you going, back to Tennessee?"

"Nope."

"Are you going after that girl you've been writing to?"

Morgan nodded. A smile broke across his face.

"I thought you might. Well, I'm headed back to Missouri. I don't know what I'll find but that's where I'm going to start. Don't forget your pass in case you run across some Feds."

Morgan stood, grasped his friend's hand, and embraced him.

"God's speed, Colter. I hope we meet again. I'll be south of Santa Fe. Don't know exactly where. If I get back as far as Tennessee, I'll try to find you."

"Same here, ole sinner. Take care."

They embraced again, pounding each other backs, and turned quickly away.

Morgan went to the livery, leading his worn-out horse. He watched the farrier forge a horseshoe and waited until the man dunked it, sizzling, into the dark water to cool. The smell of hot metal rose in a cloud of steam.

"Hello, sir. I'm looking for a mount."

"What we have is out back."

Morgan walked through the barn and studied the few horses in the corral. He stepped through the rails and slowly approached a young dun who eyed him warily and sidled away. The gelding was thin and unshod, without saddle marks.

"Can this one be ridden?"

"I can ride him. I don't know what you can do."

Morgan looked hard at him but decided that he needed the horse more than he needed a fight.

"How much would you give me for my horse? I'm going to be traveling some and I need a fresh mount."

"I'll take him for ten."

"How much for the dun and you shoe him?"

"Forty-five with your horse. Specie or greenbacks. No Confederate."

"Kind of steep, isn't it?" Morgan said as he calculated how much he would have left to get him to New Mexico.

"He hasn't been here long enough to annoy me."

Recognizing the implied threat, Morgan said, "I'll take him. When will he be ready?"

"Around noon, tomorrow."

Morgan paid the reticent man and went to gather what supplies he could find.

It'll be a light travel. I need ammunition. Maybe a fishing line and hooks.

Entering the mercantile he was greeted by an amiable young man.

"Good day, sir, how may I help you?"

Morgan greeted the man.

"I need to pick up some things for the trail," he said, as he gathered what he could find and approached the counter.

"Do you have any 56 rim fire cartridges?"

"I have a small tin of shells but not the loading box."

"That will work. I can load manually just fine."

Disconnecting the gold chain from his father's watch, he gestured to the items in front of him.

"How much will this cover?"

The bespectacled man examined the chain and said,

"I sure would like the watch that goes with this."

"I can't do that. It's my father's watch."

"Well then, another three should call us even."

Morgan pulled out some unglued stamps and handed them to the man, "Will you take postal stamps?"

"Haven't seen much of that out here. Where are you from?'

"I've been in Louisiana and East Texas. People are using stamps for money out there."

The man looked over the stamps and reluctantly said, "I guess that will be fine. I just hope I don't get burned on these."

"I don't think you will. I traded my tobacco allowance to a sutler for them."

The next morning, Morgan rolled his bedroll, stuffed his few belongings into his haversack, said his goodbyes and headed for the livery.

He settled his rope around the colt's neck and leaned back with the rope wrapped around his hip while the horse struggled to escape. Morgan slowly walked up the rope until he could touch the quivering animal. He rubbed it before slipping the bridle in his mouth. He lifted the blanket to the horse's back and carefully smoothed it, knowing that a wrinkle now would be a saddle-sore tonight. Moving slowly, he lifted his saddle and settled it on the skittish dun. *So far so good.*

As he stepped into the saddle, the dun crow-hopped and then reared, pawing the air. Morgan grabbed the saddle horn. Reaching up with the reins in his fist, he rapped the dun between the ears, driving him back to earth. The horse continued to buck and alternate kicking high with leaps and twists. *This horse has some tricks and is going to use them all.* The dun jumped high and drove his feet hard into the earth. He went to his knees and Morgan kicked loose from the stirrups.

Morgan stepped out of the saddle as the dun rolled over. The horse attempted to rise and Morgan pulled the reins around to the side, forcing the horse's head back so that he could not stand. He held him there until the gelding quit kicking and laid his head on the ground.

Loosening the reins, Morgan stepped back into the saddle as he released the head and let the animal rise. The morning passed as they tested each other, taking the measure, learning.

When they were both caked with sweat and dirt, they stood, man atop horse, trembling with exhaustion. Morgan looked through a cloud of dust to find that a crowd had gathered. He could hear a round of clapping and hoots of appreciation. He nodded and asked the grinning man standing by the gate to open it. The man tipped his hat in appreciation of the horsemanship and swung the gate wide enough for the rider and horse to pass, closing it quickly on the charging horses. Morgan raised a hand in salute and turned his new trail companion to the Rio Grande, heading north towards the girl with the stormy blue eyes.

In order to supplement his short rations with an occasional fish, he followed the river. After days with little fare in his pack, he was excited when he came across a small deer grazing under the cottonwoods on the banks of the river. He stepped off the dun and tied him securely to a tree. Jacking a shell into the chamber caused the deer to look up and freeze. Morgan drew a bead and released his breath. One shot dropped the young buck and Morgan pulled his knife from his haversack. He stroked the young horse and said, "Very good, old son. Not boogery under fire. I think your name is Walker. We have a long way to walk."0

After dressing out the deer, he dried the strips of venison over the fire. He ate his fill, wrapped his bandana around the remainder and stuffed it in a saddle bag.

Saddle sore and dusty, Morgan rocked gently to the rhythm of the tired dun as he rode down the narrow street of the small town. His hat was pulled down to shield his sore eyes from the burning sun. People turned to watch the weary stranger as he continued the length of the street. The exhausted horse stumbled and Morgan touched his spurs to his sides, reminding him to pick up his feet. He nodded slightly to each person who met his gaze, knowing how leery they all must be to see another straggler pass through their town. He was only slightly aware of the sideways glances as he looked for the livery stable and a barber shop. The horse picked up his pace as Morgan pointed the trail-worn horse toward the large wooden barn and corrals.

Morgan put his mount in the corral and paid the liveryman for feed and water. Not ready to talk to anyone, he headed to the barber shop for a bath and shave. He listened to a group of men in the shop comparing the strengths and speed of two horses. "I don't care what you say, my black can outrun your bay any day of the week."

"If Gordon weren't ridin' him you'd not have won. He rides on the track."

"I'll tell you what, Tillman, let's match up again and Gordon kin ride yer bay and you kin ride the black. I'm bettin' he still wins. Half a horse race is the rider."

The men exited the shop, still arguing the merits of horses and riders. Morgan thought about what had been said and wished he had the time to view that horse race. The conversation reminded him of the track that his father had scraped out of their pasture in Tennessee and how his father had taught him to ride.

He bathed and put on a relatively clean set of clothes. He asked the barber for directions to a boarding house and soon found a room for the night. It was hard to get comfortable in the straw bed after sleeping for weeks on the ground. Tossing in the crackling straw soon turned into heavy slumber as weeks on the trail drained away.

Soon enough the light slipped under the quilt tacked to the window and woke Morgan. He rolled to the edge of the bed and pulled on his boots. Gathering his gear, he headed for the livery.

A short, heavyset man studied Morgan as he approached. "Hello, soldier. Are you looking for employment?"

"Well, I don't have any," Morgan said, studying the well-dressed gentleman.

"I have a ranch about an hour out of town. Rafter R. I need some help, all around. Thirty and found. My name is David Randel."

"Well, sir, I'm pretty good at all around."

"Where are you from?"

"Had a place in Tennessee, then went to Texas."

"You in the army? I see you're wearing a cavalry cap."

"I fought at Glorieta Pass and then went back to Texas for a couple of years."

"You men got your asses handed to you, didn't you?" The man's belly jumped up and down as he laughed at his own joke. "I'm loading supplies. Meet me at The Capitol and I'll stake you to a meal before we head out."

Morgan saluted him and went to get his horse. *Thirty and found. Not the best offer I've heard of but then I probably won't have to kill anybody. And close enough to start looking for that Sophia. Things are looking up!"*

Morgan rode beside the buckboard, answering David Randel's questions but sharing little else until they reached the ranch. He was relieved when the conversation turned from the war to ranch business. The morning sun had burned off any coolness from the night when Mr. Randel drove in with the stranger. Parnell rode up and greeted them, sizing up the rider and his gear. Morgan knew that he looked saddle worn, drawn. Parnell looked hard in the man's eyes. Morgan met his gaze without blinking.

"Morning, Mr. Randel. Coffee is still hot in the shack. Cookie can rustle up some grub if you want something. I sent the men to look for the cat."

"We're fine. Parnell, this is Morgan. Use him where you need him. Said he used to break horses."

"I'll show him the bunk house."

Parnell started for the bunk house without looking to see if Morgan followed. Morgan stepped into the quarters behind the ranch foreman. "This is your bunk. Zeke sleeps close to Corky so he can kick him when he snores. He might want to change bunks with you. You look like military," Parnell said, glancing at Morgan's hat. "Don't start anything."

"I was and I won't," Morgan said, briefly.

"There's two colts in the corral. Saddles in the tack room if you don't want to use yours for rough stock."

Morgan nodded and stepped aside as Parnell exited through the open door. Morgan closed the door and looked around. He noted the boot jack fashioned from a branch by the door and the black, cast-iron Ben Franklin in the corner. A rough-hewn table and four mismatched chairs stood in the middle of the room. A well-thumbed deck of cards sat in the middle of the old table. He decided that the bunk house did not look that much different than the barracks in San Antonio.

Morgan placed his saddlebags and bedroll on the straw mattress, dug his money out of a leather case and rolled it tightly, stuffing it in the coin bag. Lifting the corner of the mat, he reached for his knife, carefully cut the stitches in the mattress, and slipped the entirety of his savings inside the cotton ticking. He pulled the precious photograph from his shirt and studied it before slipping it into the mattress.

This will do just fine. Time to earn my keep. Morgan found the worn-out Mc-Clellan saddles and one Clarke saddle with a broken tree in the barn. *I believe there will be less bone rattling if I use my own.* He spent the afternoon smoothing out the wrinkles in the young horses and soon heard the dinner bell. Morgan made a place for his rigging and looked for a place to wash up. Joining the men at the shack, he noticed that two men were sitting on the bench and Parnell was sitting in a chair.

He started to sit in the vacant chair but the motionless silence warned him that he had done something wrong. Parnell said, "Morgan this is Zeke, Corky and Cookie. That chair is Cookie's. Use the other bench."

Morgan nodded at the men and said nothing, trying to figure the pecking order and where he would fit in.

"Anything to do around here for entertainment?"

"Not much. We need to sort the heavy springers and get them moved. They need to be closer to headquarters so the big cats don't get the calves. Corky and Zeke are trying to find a catamount that is settled by the north water.

Parnell turned to Morgan. "Can you track?"

"I've done a bit."

"Help Zeke and Corky move those springers first. We don't want to have to ride the far pastures, guarding calves. There's going to be a gathering at the Chatham ranch in two weeks. I guess everyone wants to go."

An enthusiastic round of yeses ensued.

Cookie stepped outside and rang the dinner bell, which hung beside the door, calling the hands to breakfast. Two chairs and two benches. There was always a race to see who got the chair when Parnell was not there.

"Mornin' Cookie."

"Mornin,' Zeke."

"Top of the mornin' to you, Cookie."

"And the rest of the day to you, Corky."

"Greetings, Parnell."

"Greetings to you, Cookie."

"Morning, Morgan."

Morgan nodded but said nothing. Sizing up the addition at the table, Cookie seemed satisfied that he would have no trouble with him and turned to the black, cast-iron stove to retrieve the platters of food. Corky, in his usual high humor, broke into song.

"As I went out through Dublin City, at the hour of twelve at night, I spied a Spanish Lady washing her feet by candlelight."

Shut up that catterwaulin' Corky. It's eatin' time," warned Parnell, keeping an eye on the cook. The quality of the meals hinged on Cookie's mood. "You know better than to upset the mules or Cookie!"

Cookie glared and nodded. He slid a platter of biscuits onto the table and Zeke, hoping to make points with the cook said, "Look at them cat heads."

Oblivious to the annoyance he had caused, Corky said, "I'll have my eggs mugged if you please, Cookie."

"You'll have 'em like I fix em, Bonehead."

"Yes sir," Corky replied as he took a long reach and stabbed a thick slice of ham.

"Yes sir, I'll be pleased with how you fix 'em and not give a toss. Look at them hind trotters," he finished as he slapped the large pink slice of ham on to his plate.

Parnell, a man of few words, looked up and caught the cook's eye.

"Laruppin' as usual, Cookie."

All the men nodded in agreement, concerned about what the cook might provide for the next meal.

Cookie tilted his head in acknowledgment, pleased that the pecking order in his kitchen had been restored. The men ate in silence, afraid to upset the delicate balance of power in his domain.

Morgan helped himself after the others, grateful for the spread but wishing that it was beef or venison instead of ham. It stunk. At least there was a substantial platter of biscuits.

When the meal was finished Parnell said, "Zeke, you and Morgan go north to the lake and cut for sign. I saw cat tracks but they were covered when I checked the waters day before yesterday. Take a couple of hunting horses and your rifles. Corky, you help me."

After Parnell gave each man his assignment for the day, they filed out the door. Zeke called over his shoulder, "What's for supper, Cookie?"

"You ain't got rid of your breakfast yet and you're already lookin' for supper!?"

"It gives me somethin' to think about during the day."

The grizzled old man relented. "Beef and beans."

"Beans, again? Can't you fix nothin' else?"

"Coffee!" the old man said and slammed the door.

Chapter 8
The Plan
2012

The familiar smell of urine and the bawl of cattle assailed Morgan as he climbed the concrete steps to the upper reaches of the Sale Barn and waved at some of his neighbors. Tom and Eldrige were seated together. Sitting with some of the men he knew, Doroteo nodded at Morgan. Travis walked in and climbed the steps to sit beside Morgan. Beyond a perfunctory greeting, they were silent. After watching the cattle sell all morning, everyone filed out of the arena to eat or have coffee, tending to their own business.

Morgan said, "Why don't we eat at the Sale Barn Cafe?"

Travis nodded and they found two empty chairs and ordered.

"That load from the B Hat looked a little light."

"Yeah, but they brought good money."

"I was hoping to pick up some lightweights for the house pasture. The grass is ready."

"You might talk to Carson. I think he's going to pull some calves soon."

"I'll do that."

The meal continued in silence until they stood to go. Maintaining the subterfuge, Morgan said, "See you later, I have to go get some salt."

"Okay. See you next week."

At two o'clock, the four men gathered at the Rancher's Cafe. Shaking hands, they sat at the far table, Morgan with his back to the wall. He watched for Doroteo. When he came in, he politely asked if he could sit with the men. Morgan nodded slightly. Everyone was playing their part well.

Without preamble, Morgan said, "Well, I think it's time we did something about the missing cattle. Doroteo has some information that I think will answer our questions. Doroteo?" Morgan turned to the old man.

"Si. I have been watching the rock house down by The River, behind the old Hudson place. It looks like three hombres pick up a large calf from someone and bring it to the house on Sunday night to kill and dress. Then early Monday morning, while you go to the Sale Barn, they cut and package it, carry off the hide. They throw the bones and stuff in The River, then take the meat somewhere to sell."

"Why would they throw stuff in The River? Why not bury it?" Eldrige queried.

"Probably so the turtles and catfish will clean it up. The muddy water will wash away the evidence. Pretty clever, actually," Travis responded.

"So, if we know this, why don't we get the Brand Inspector to take care of it?" Tom asked.

"Because I don't know where Hilario stands on this. He hasn't been an Inspector for very long. And you know that Greg Carrasco is dirty."

"Yeah. He's a big fish in a dirty pond," said Eldrige.

"Right. He's the crookedest deputy in the Sheriff Department. Here's what I think we should do if we all agree. We go confront them when they least expect it. I think we can scare them off if everyone is agreed," Morgan suggested.

Everyone nodded agreement.

"Okay, then. On Monday, instead of going to the sale, Travis and I will go in from his River pasture, park the truck and ride in behind the house. Eldrige and Tom, you park up by the highway so they don't see any dust and ride to the east and west corners of the house. Doroteo, if you want to, and everyone will understand if you don't, you go to the front door. But not before we surround the house."

"Aiii," the man said, twisting his furrowed brown face in disapproval.

"That's fine, Doroteo. We understand. You don't want any trouble with them. Eldrige can translate. Okay, Eldrige?"

"Yep."

After making plans for the following Monday Morgan said, "Well boys, that's about it. Keep it under your hats." Tom, Eldrige, Travis and Morgan lifted their hats in unison. Doroteo looked at the men. Although not understanding the gesture, he lifted his. They all replaced their hats and rose.

As they left the table, Morgan determined to follow up on something else Doroteo had said. The other men had laughed at the tale, but it struck a nerve with Morgan. Doroteo described an old man living down River who spoke about coming across from the other side a long time ago. Tom said the man must be demented. Morgan was not so sure. Doroteo said that he told old stories and talked different. *Could this man have crossed from the past as I've done. Maybe he knows something more about The River than I do.*

The next morning, Morgan ate breakfast, fixed a sandwich, and filled a thermos with yesterday's tea. Going to the barn, he found his saddlebags and carried them to the house. He slipped his sandwich and tea into one pocket and looked around for some supplies to take as a gift to Charlie Dunn. He bagged coffee, salt and flour from their larger containers and stuffed these things in the saddle bags. Grabbing his rifle and jacket, he carried everything to the barn. His hunting horse nickered a greeting, anxious for a flake of hay. He put the saddlebags and rifle in the truck and tossed hay to the horse. He set the gear on the fence rail and brushed the gelding.

By the time everything was situated, Hunter was cleaning up the last wisps of hay. Morgan saddled the horse, loaded him in the trailer and slipped behind the wheel. Following the directions that Doroteo had offered, Morgan followed the highway south to the third county crossroad. He turned down the dusty road along a fence marked with BLM signs. The notice at the cattle guard said, "County Road. Not Maintained." He pulled off the road and cut the engine.

"Better unload my all-terrain vehicle." Morgan said, chuckling at his own joke. He opened the tailgate, patted the hind quarter of the tall gelding, and told him to step back. The horse gingerly felt for the ground and stepped down from the trailer. Morgan tied him to the tailgate. Reaching into the truck, he lifted out the saddlebags and rifle and settled them on the saddle.

He took a bite of his sandwich and studied the line of trees which traced the curve of The River. Finishing the thermos of tea, Morgan tightened the cinch and swung easily into the saddle. He turned the horse south and began a slow lope toward the trees. Slowing to a walk, he lifted his head and sniffed the air, searching for any sign of human habitation.

The familiar scent of the muddy River wafted towards him, slightly fishy and salty from the tamarack trees. He urged Hunter to a trot along the tree line, stopping occasionally to check the air for any other smells. The salt cedars were throwing shadows across his path by the time Morgan smelled the wood smoke of a campfire. Slowing to a walk he called, "Hello, the camp." The birds silenced and he listened through the stillness. He moved out of the shadows and continued further south.

"Hello, the camp," he called again.

Morgan reined the gelding to a stop when he noticed a gray, ragged man watching him from the shadows, a rifle anchored against his hip. When the old man realized that Morgan had spotted him, he said, "Whadda ya want?"

Morgan put both hands on the pommel of the saddle, showing that he was unarmed. The old man eyed the rifle in the scabbard under Morgan's leg and repeated, "Whadda ya want?"

"I'm looking for a man named Charlie Dunn. Would that be you?"

"Might be. Who are ya and I'll ask ya one more time, stranger, whadda ya want?"

"My apologies sir. My name is Donnally. Morgan Donnally. I was told that you might have some information I'm looking for. I brought you some supplies. Salt, flour, coffee."

"Real coffee?"

"Real coffee."

"Wa'll, light down. I guess it won't hurt to jaw a bit."

"Will do."

The old man took the supplies and stashed them inside the half dugout before emerging with a pot and the bag of coffee. He dipped water into the pot from a large bucket hanging from a beam. With unwashed hands, he pinched coffee grounds from the bag and carefully sprinkled them into the pot on a hanger. Removing strips of venison from the branch perched over the hot ashes, he spun the hook over the coals, threw more small branches in the fire, and stirred the flames.

Morgan tied his horse and waited, giving the man time to make up his mind about the situation. Having adjusted the wood every way he could, the old man said, in a voice unused to speech, "Whadda ya want?"

"Well, sir, I was told that you may have come from across The River and I'd like to know if that's true."

The hermit looked up quickly, scanning Morgan's face.

Realizing that the grizzled man might not be willing to talk and afraid of losing this one opportunity, Morgan chose his words carefully, speaking slowly so the man would have time to understand exactly what he was saying.

"Doroteo Remundo. Do you remember him?"

The old man nodded slowly, fidgeting.

"Well, Doroteo is a friend of mine. He mentioned that you might have come from across The River a long time ago. I did, too. I was hoping we could talk about it."

Morgan stopped, letting that sink in. The man rose and went into the hut. Morgan squatted, hunkered down, afraid to move and not knowing what to expect. In a few minutes, the old gent returned with a cup made from a tin can with a wire tied around the top and bottom rim. In the other hand, a bowl scraped from a piece of mesquite.

He handed Morgan the bowl and said, by way of explanation, "I don't get company."

With a piece of hide in hand, he took the pot from the hook and poured Morgan a bowl of coffee and filled his own tin cup.

"What are ya doin' on this side?"

Morgan began his tale with the day he was looking for cattle and found Leland drowning in The River. The old man nodded but said nothing. His story spun itself out and he sat, silent, watching the old man.

"Want some jerky ta go with that coffee?"

"Proud to."

Morgan reached out, took the proffered meat strip, and held up his bowl for more coffee. They chewed in silence as both men thought his own thoughts and took the measure of each other.

Much time passed before the old man spoke again. "My name's Dunn. Charlie Dunn. I come across some years back. I crossed at a horseshoe bend up River. Water was up. My horse slipped and I ended up on this side. Lost my horse. Fer a long time I didn't know this side was different. I found a settlement. The people were strange. Everythin'."

"I understand that. Why are you out here, if you don't mind me asking?"

"Don't guess I do. I got in some trouble with the law so I come out here so's I would be left alone." He glanced sideways at Morgan. "I heerd stories 'bout men going back and forth. I didn't."

"It must be solitare out here. Didn't you ever think about going back?"

"Nope. Didn't have a horse and can't swim. Didn't leave nothin' over there. Been livin' here ever since."

Morgan waited for him to continue but silence filled the space between them. Soon the only sound was the chittering of birds settling in for the night and the ba-ruk of frogs. The darkness slipped through the trees. Apparently, the old man was finished. Morgan sat on a log and stared into the dying embers. Charlie swung the venison rack over the coals, replaced the strips, and sat back against a large flat rock.

Morgan studied the profile of the old man in the firelight. He looked like an old saddle tramp. Like the men who were homeless after the war and drifted from camp to camp looking for a meal or lodging. The long, limp hair fell in a gray mat on bony shoulders covered with a faded blue shirt. One button was missing at the sunken belly, leaving a gap where the folds of loose flesh poked through. The threadbare trousers were tucked into a pair of run over boots, scratched and scuffed, worn nearly white. The next words sounded like they had been drug across a gravel road.

"If ya go across, fork a stout horse."

"Thanks, pardner."

Morgan waited, hoping that the man would offer some other knowledge. The only sound was the crackle of the dying fire.

"Well, I'm pleased to meet you, Charlie Dunn. I better head out."

There was no response. Morgan rose. The conversation was over. Morgan untied the horse and swung into the saddle.

"Thanks for the talk and chew."

"Thanks for the supplies."

Morgan saluted, turned his horse, and gave the gelding his head, comfortable that the trail wise animal would find the trailer in the rapidly fading light.

It was full dark when Morgan arrived home, penned the horse, tossed hay in the feeder, and headed for the house. Entering the dark kitchen, he flipped the light switch and called for Jake. Finishing his duties, he poured himself a drink and sat in his favorite chair.

Soon his thoughts wound backward, like a clock erasing time. Memories filled his head and roiled his emotions. He sat, staring into the blankness, seeing nothing but visions of her as they talked and danced and made love so long ago. He squeezed his eyes shut, preventing the moisture that welled up. He stood and went to pour himself another drink, his thoughts churning inside of him, coiling tightly around his heart. He had loved Sophia so long ago and he loved Carolina now. The daughter of his deceased wife. She had become like a daughter to him. The clash of old life and new clanged in his head. The old love still burned in him, inflaming his mind. He was torn between duty to Carolina, the child he had raised, and Sophia.

So long ago and Sophia still walked around in the corners of his mind, now more than ever, turning him inside out. He knew the way back now, dangerous as it was. Morgan quickly emptied the bourbon in his glass and poured another one. Deliberately, counting his breaths, trying to slow the beating of his heart, he weighed the cost, the possibilities.

He would go back across The River. He only needed to see her. He needed to know what had happened to her. He understood now that he could only cross over when The River was at flood stage, in the horseshoe bend of The River. A dangerous, uncertain undertaking. No guarantee that he could get back to her. The memory of her heated up his brain. Could he even get back to the same place?

He was tired of living like this. Morgan curled his hand and rubbed the stubble on his jaw. *I'm not getting any younger. Carolina needs to take responsibility for this ranch. It's hers. She can do what she wants with it. It's time to choose the regret that I can live with.* Visions of the little curly-haired girl that he raised crowded his mind's eye. *I did my best for her and I did right by her mother, but now, for whatever time I have left, if I can get back to Sophia that's what I want to do.*

He drained the drink and walked the kitchen floor. As he reached to pour himself another, he found that there was nothing left. Morgan held up the Seagram's bottle, surprised that it was empty. He paced back and forth. The tension in him built until the room could not contain him. Stepping outside, he let the door slam behind him. The memory of her was making him crazy. The years with Carolina and Veronica slipped away and he was thirty again, and in love with Sophia.

To Hell with it!! He reached inside the door and grabbed his hat and truck keys from the sideboard. Twisting his hat down tight on his head as though he was preparing to ride a bronc, he got in the truck and started driving toward Dickson. The night air cleared his head and he realized that he better not go into town. *Maybe just stop by the No Name Saloon and listen to the band. Am I going crazy? What else can I do on this side of The River?*

As Morgan opened the door to the bar, he heard the band tuning up.

"Some of you may not know us. We're the Cheerful Cowboys. We aim to put a smile on your faces. Some of you might have come here to cry in your beer or fight. Please don't. It'll spoil the mood. Let your hair down if you have any and let's get started."

As the music filled the large dance hall, he found a stool at the bar and ordered a Seagram's and water. The bartender nodded and, putting a napkin down in front of Morgan, reached across the bar with the amber-filled glass. He slowly centered the drink on the paper square and studied the tall man.

Morgan met his gaze, knowing that the bartender was looking for signs of impairment. He stared moodily at the bar top as he finished the whiskey. He ordered another as a woman appeared at his shoulder. Her teased, bleached hair framed a thin face with traces of age around her mouth. Her moist brown eyes, shadowed in bronze, looked up at him, invitingly. With a generous smile she said, "Hi, I'm Darlene. How about a dance, cowboy?"

He studied the woman from the corner of his eye. Her fitted white shirt was tucked into a pair of suitably faded blue jeans. He noted that she was wearing what some of the cowboys called "passion boots." High heel boots which thrust her breasts forward and tipped her backend up in the air, like a cat in heat.

He turned his head to her and said, "Sorry, I didn't come here to dance."

"Of course not," she parried. "That's because you didn't know that I would be here."

Morgan twisted around to face her, amused by her quick reply. Finishing the drink, he stood looking down at her and said, "I surely did not. Let's try a round." He pushed his hat to the back of his head.

As they moved to the dance floor, he held her with room between them. She slowly moved closer until they were touching. He stiffened his arms to keep the distance between them. Memories of holding Sofia swept like a hot wind through his brain. He maneuvered the woman until they were once again danc-ing apart. The nearness of this willing woman muddied up his memories, con-fused his thoughts. She moved close to him again, stirring up hungers in him for a woman which mixed with old emotions.

Thoughts of Sophia merged with the woman in his arms. He pulled her closer, their bodies moving in harmony until the music stopped. Morgan con-tinued to hold her tight against him as the other couples left the floor. Stepping back, Darlene said "Whoa, cowboy, we're just dancing, right now."

He stared down at her, weighing the implication of her words, and said in a voice low and hoarse with desire, "You started it."

"I just meant not now."

"How about a drink?"

She nodded and he said, "Let's find a table. Old man, old manners." She looked at him, puzzled by his words. Even in his inebriated state, he would not let a lady sit at the bar with him.

Darlene sipped her drink as they talked. Morgan downed his and gestured for another. She studied him closely, asking question after question and receiv-ing vague answers. Giving up, she reached out, patted his hand and said,

"It's obvious that you have something or someone on your mind. I'm going to leave you with it. Thanks for the drink and the dance, cowboy, maybe I'll see you again." He nodded silently, touching the brim of his hat as he rose to re-claim his stool at the bar.

Looking at the bartender, he said, "Barkeep, do it again." The man shook his head slightly and in a conciliatory voice said, "Friend, you don't want me to get in trouble and I don't want you to get in trouble so how about you getting some fresh air?"

Morgan's face tightened and he closed his fists. A desire to hurt someone, anyone, welled up in him. The loneliness and frustration needing an outlet.

The bartender gestured to the bouncers by the door.

"Buddy, don't do it," indicating the men who had suddenly appeared at Morgan's elbows.

Morgan looked to his right and left. He nodded. Holding up his hands in acquiescence, he tugged his hat down tight on his head, swung around, and headed unsteadily toward the door. Finding his pickup, he fumbled with his keys, beeping open the lock. Crawling behind the wheel, he tried to focus his eyes on the flashing sign above the bar. In slow motion, Morgan slid sideways and fell asleep on the leather seat of his new pickup, in the dusty parking lot.

Morgan woke as the morning sun melted the night sky. He eased himself upright, testing the damage he had done the night before. Nothing broken, cotton mouth and a fevered brain pushing his eyeballs out of his head. *Damn! I've done smarter things than this.* He started the truck and turned on the AC, directing the cool air to his face. With fingers massaging his temples, he sat perfectly still, contemplating his next move. Recalling the jug of water in the back floorboard, he stepped out of the truck, and found the plastic jug. Turning it up, he drained the stale, warm water down his parched throat. As he eased back under the wheel, a pair of old boots on the floorboard reminded him of an errand he might run, so the day and the gas would not be a total waste. Gingerly, he pointed the truck toward Dickson, wishing he had a cold drink of something to wash the taste of dead cat from his mouth.

Morgan parked the truck and slid slowly along the seat of the pickup. He reached down and picked up the worn boots, squeezing his eyes closed against the pain. He backed out of the truck holding his head steady. Looking around, he crossed the street and stepped onto the sidewalk, amused as he watched a small boy swaggering up and down in front of the store window, scrutinizing his own small reflection. The child spied Morgan closing the distance between them. His eyes widened in disbelief, looking up at the man approaching. Morgan soon towered over him. When he realized that he had the man's undivided attention the boy whispered, "Are you a real cowboy, mister?"

"Well, pardner, that's for others to say, not me. That's what I aim for. My name's Morgan, what's yours?"

"My name is Phillip."

Morgan hunkered down to the boy's level and spoke face to face, wincing at the pounding in his head. "Glad to meet you, Phillip. You're not from around here, are you? Where are you from?"

"We came to see my aunt Eda. We came from Chicago."

"Well, that's a good place to come from. Where's your mom, Phillip?"

"She's shopping. She's taking a long time. I don't like to shop."

"Me either, Phillip, but I like to eat. Sometimes we have to do things we don't like in order to get what we do like; don't you think?"

"I guess so. What are you doing?"

"I'm going to get these boots half-soled. Save myself a few greenbacks. Then I'm going to pick up some mineral blocks for the cattle."

"What are greenbacks?"

"Dollars. Dollars are green."

Appearing to lose interest in the conversation the boy said, "I like to eat. I better go help my mom."

"Nice to meet you, Phillip. You have a good day."

"You too, sir."

Morgan entered the boot shop and greeted the old German with a leather apron tied around him.

"Morning, Gunerson."

"Morning to you, Donnally. What can I do for you?"

"Don't know if it will do any good but I thought I would get these half-soled and see how long they'll last."

"Never hurts to try, does it? I don't understand how a man who rides a horse for a living can wear out the soles of his boots."

"Well, once you do the mounted work, you have to get off and do the groundwork. Then you get cleaned up and give the girls a whirl."

"Any one in particular?"

"Not a one. When can I get these back?"

"Next week good enough?"

"I'll be here Monday afternoon." Morgan knew full well that they would not be ready on Monday but if he did not come in and remind the crusty old man, they would never get done at all.

Morgan walked back down the street, got in the pickup, and drove to the feed store. The big green sign read Dickson Feed and Seed.

He studied the trays of gangly tomato and pepper plants and the flowers. The proprietor was spraying a mist over them.

"Morning, Hiriam. How're you doin' this morning?"

"Better than you, probably."

"Oh?"

"Saw you at the No Name last night. You really tied one on."

"I got started early."

"I'll say. I thought you was goin' to tangle with those boys."

Morgan crooked his head in reply and changed the subject. "I need a dozen mineral blocks, Hiriam. Throw on a couple bags of dog food and put it on the ranch account. Are those lavender plants?"

"Yes, indeedy. Just got them in. Do great here but don't over water them."

"I'll take two."

"Will do. Pull around to the back and I'll get you loaded." Hiriam turned off the water and trailed through the store, carrying the lavender plants.

Morgan reached into his pocket and pulled out enough change to feed the large, red, Coca-Cola box. Choosing a water, he said peevishly, "Seems a shame to pay for water, Hiriam."

"Got to pay for the delivery system, Morgan."

"S'pose so, Hiriam. S'pose so." He mused. Do you have any gum or mints or something?"

Hiriam gauged the condition of the tall man and handed him a package of gum, saying, "On the house, Morgan."

"Thanks."

Morgan returned to the ranch and sat in the truck, waiting for the pounding in his head to ease. He pushed at his eyes as if to keep them in his head. They still ached, blurring his vision. He eased himself out of the truck and tossed flakes of hay in the feeder for the colt he was breaking, his hunting horse and the old dun. He transferred the mineral blocks to the work truck. Shouldering the sacks of dog food, he headed for the house.

Too early to go to bed and too late to get started on anything worthwhile, Morgan went to the kitchen. Searching the cupboards, he remembered that he had emptied the bottle of whiskey the night before. *Damn!* He made a pot of coffee and, carrying a mug to the front porch, sat with his heels propped on the railing.

Again, his thoughts ran back to that time on The River.

Chapter 9
Remembering the River Incident
2012

His horse had followed him across the churning water and, after Morgan caught him, stood nervously as Morgan helped the spent man into the soggy saddle. Fishing in his pocket, he pulled out his father's watch and opened it. He shook it and blew out the drops of muddy water that had seeped into the case. He kept blowing on it as they slowly made their way in the direction the man indicated. As his leg warmed, the throbbing from the horse kick grew until his entire leg swelled and pulsed with pain. The afternoon sun was sliding into the western haze when he spotted a rock house in the distance. By the time darkness had settled on the ranch, they had reached the filtered light in the front window.

"Hello, the house," Morgan called out, surprised at the croak in his parched throat.

A tall, dark-headed woman appeared at the opened door and seeing her husband, rushed to him with a small cry. Morgan helped the man down and half-carried, half-dragged him as the woman directed him into the house, to the quilt-covered bed in the first bedroom. He laid the heaving body gently on the bed and stepped back, awaiting further instructions.

"May I help, Ma'am?"

"My name is Veronica. This is Leland, my husband. I'll take care of him. Please put your horse in the corral and come back."

"My name is Donnally, Morgan Donnally."

She glanced up but did not respond.

He unsaddled his horse and tossed him some hay, broken from the tight bales tied with an orange cord. A quick glance at the water tank showed that it was full. He looked around in the gathering dark, unable to make out much except the neglect of the house. Stepping through the door, he quietly leaned against the door frame, watching the woman bathe the now nearly naked man.

She looked up and noticing Morgan, asked if he would get a glass of water. He searched the kitchen and after some time found that the tap at the sink would bring forth water when the handle was turned. He filled a glass from the drainboard and returned to her. The cotton dress clung to her broad shoulders and round hips. Her long legs were exposed as she bent over the man. *Mercy! That was a short dress.* He couldn't help admiring the exposed, shapely legs, even now, remembering.

A child of five appeared at the bedside, awakened by the lights and voices. She was crying and holding her father's hand. Throwing herself on the man's chest, she wailed, "Daddy, don't die! Please don't die."

Veronica turned to Morgan, pleading silently for help. He reached for the little girl and lifted her against him. Cradling her head against his chest, Morgan said, "Let's leave your mother to take care of your daddy. He'll be fine. He just needs some rest." Morgan had been with the man all day. He was certain that the man would not be fine but there was no point in riding the broom on him.

Morgan sat with the tiny girl on his lap, stroking her head until she exhausted herself with tears.

"My name is Morgan Donnally, what's yours?"

"Carolina," she sniffed.

Morgan held her, gently rocking until she fell asleep. Rising slowly, so as not to wake her, he found her bedroom down the hall and, lowering the still form into the quilts, he murmured into her ear as she fidgeted against her pillow. He studied the sleeping child, sorry for what he knew was coming, wanting to protect her from the grief.

As he stood in the doorway, Morgan watched Veronica talk to her husband, wiping the mud from his mouth each time he coughed. She was calm and her tears fell silently on the man's bare chest as she tended him, unaware of Morgan's presence. She gently turned the man on his side and adjusted his shoulders so he could spit out the muddy vomit.

"Shall I make some coffee?"

"Thank you. There's some on the counter in the kitchen."

Looking around, he noticed the white, electric coffee maker with a glass carafe sitting on the counter. He remembered how unsettling all these things were when he had first encountered them. Finding two china cups, he filled them and returned to the bedroom.

The woman reached for the telephone and spoke into it with some urgency. "This is Veronica Thompson. My husband has almost drowned in The River. I'm bringing him in." She then turned to Morgan and asked, "Will you help me get him into the truck?" Morgan followed her lead and helped her drag the man out the back door and into the pickup. He offered to stay with the little girl. The woman nodded and slid behind the wheel of the truck. They were soon out of sight.

He remembered thinking that he was in a strange world that somehow had something to do with The River. He needed to get back down there and sort things out, but for the moment he had made a promise.

Morgan woke the next morning with the remembered ache of sleeping on an Army cot. The familiar sensation of pain in his leg brought him back to the moment. He lifted his head and looked around. He was in a small barn. He remembered finding his way out here when Veronica returned from the hospital. Attempting to rise from the cot, he looked down at the contusion on his thigh and sat rubbing it, stirring blood back into his leg. He fumbled from the cot and looked for his clothes. They were crusted with mud and stiff. He wiggled into them and found his boots under the cot. *Better find a way to clean these first.*

Sticking his head out of the door, he saw Walker staring at the barn. The horse whinnied when he spotted Morgan walking gingerly, in his stocking feet, to the corral. He turned the boots upside down, poured the water out and washed the mud from them the best he could. They were still soggy when he tugged them on. He remembered the hay in the barn, retrieved some for Walker and headed for the house.

Veronica emerged from the doorway, as she had the night before, and greeted him.

"Did you sleep well, Mr. Donnally?"

"Yes, ma'am I did. How's your husband?"

"It doesn't look good. He swallowed a lot of muddy water, and the doctor is afraid of pneumonia."

"I'm sorry to hear that, ma'am. Is there anything I can do to help?"

"First thing is, call me Veronica."

"Yes, ma'am. Veronica," he corrected himself.

"Why don't you come in and have some breakfast. I called the hospital. There isn't any change. I am going back when we finish eating."

Morgan followed her into the house and sat down to a pile of pancakes and bacon.

She poured him a cup of coffee and he ate silently until she began to question him. *I better keep things to myself until I figure out what the hell is going on.* The strangeness of the situation befuddled him.

"Where are you from, Mr. Donnally?"

"I'm from Tennessee but I've been in these parts for a while. And you should call me Morgan."

"What did you do in Tennessee, Morgan?"

"My dad and I raised horses."

Knowing that staying any longer would lead to more questions, Morgan excused himself and left the table. He went outside and looked toward The River.

Veronica joined him on the porch, towing Carolina.

"You are welcome to stay here unless you have some place to be."

"I don't, ma'am."

"Veronica," she corrected. "Make yourself at home. I don't know when we'll be back.

Morgan nodded, anxious to see what it would take for him to get back across The River. He watched them drive off and went inside to see what food he could find to take with him. He found a loaf of bread and a package of deli meat. He made himself two sandwiches. Spying a kitchen towel hung on the stove, he wrapped the sandwiches, grabbed an apple, and took everything to the barn. After shaking out the water, he stowed them in the soggy saddlebags.

Searching around, he located a rag and a can of saddle soap. He took these things to the corral and began to clean his saddle and horse. By late morning, he mounted Walker and headed for The River.

Three hours of riding brought him to edge of The River. He sat horseback and studied the fast, roiling water. *How did we even make it? The Good Lord must have had a Hand in it.* He shook his head in amazement and could feel his stomach knot with the fear he felt when he went into that muddy, red water.

Morgan began looking for signs where he and Leland had come out of the water.

Another hour brought him to the spot where he had dragged the man up the embankment and the hoof and boot prints where he loaded him on Walker. He dismounted and pulled off the boots which were pinching his feet. He soaked them in The River and then packed them tightly with sand. He ate the sandwiches and tied the boots to his saddle horn, mounted and turned Walker towards the house.

Morgan heard the truck in the yard and hurried in his stocking feet to meet Veronica and Carolina. Veronica stepped down from the truck, tears coursing down her cheeks, and reached for her child. Morgan said, "I'll get her."

Veronica nodded and slipped into the house. The sleeping child snuggled against Morgan and reached her arms around his neck when he lifted her from the car seat.

After settling her into bed Morgan went outside, not knowing what else to do. Veronica joined him on the front porch and handed him a cup of coffee. Without preamble, she said, "I don't think he's going to make it. He looks worse and has a fever."

"I am very sorry to hear that, Veronica."

She slipped her arm though his and buried her face in the sleeve of his dirty shirt. He reached with the other hand and stroked her hair until she quit crying.

Veronica gave Morgan some clothes from Leland's closet. Thanking her, he went to change into the clean clothes. He poured the dry sand out of his boots, pulled them on and found that they now fit him better.

The funeral was a small affair, attended by the local ranching families. They looked sideways at Morgan. He introduced himself as the hired hand. Morgan took the little girl for a long walk and returned carrying her, with her face buried in his neck.

When everyone left, Morgan began to tidy up the house, leaving Veronica to tend to her child. Carolina was becoming angry and disobedient. Veronica screamed at her and threw her on her bed. "Stay there until you can behave!"

The child wailed and ran to Morgan. Not knowing what to do, he picked her up and put an arm around Veronica. "Let's go for a walk."

As the days went by, Morgan mediated between mother and child while they grieved and fought and established a way to live without father and husband. Veronica cooked and taught Carolina while Morgan found things to clean or repair around the house and barn. In the afternoons, he saddled Walker and rode to The River. When the water started to recede, he told Veronica that he might be leaving.

"I didn't plan to stay, Veronica."

"But you said that you didn't have any place to be. Why not be here? I can pay you a little and you will have room and board."

"I need to get back where I came from."

Her stricken look tugged at him. He looked away and walked to the barn.

Morgan rode away in the morning, before Veronica arose. He knew that Carolina would cry, but she wasn't his, as precious as she was.

He found the place where he had crossed and slowly eased the nervous horse into the water. The horse climbed up the embankment and Morgan stopped to look around. *It's not the same. The trees and grass look different. Even the cattle are different. Black and short legged. Not like the range cows I was chasing when I went into the water.*

Soon he came to a wire fence and rode along, looking for a gate. A No Trespassing sign stopped him. *None of this is right.* A fence, as far as he could see before The River made a bend. Morgan turned back to The River and slowly eased across.

He saw them before they spotted him. Veronica was standing, leaning against a post, in the shadows of the front porch. Her arms hugged her chest and Carolina's arms wrapped around her mother with her face buried in her mother's hip. When they saw him returning, Veronica unfurled her arms and wiped her face with both hands. Carolina let out a cry and ran to him.

Morgan dismounted, holding the reins and gathered the child in his arms.

"Just went for a ride," he said.

"I'm glad you're back."

Carolina planted a noisy kiss on his cheek.

They fell into a routine as the weeks went by. Morgan worked around the place in the morning while Veronica spent time with Carolina. He rode across The River every afternoon to see if anything had changed. Nothing had.

Morgan began to spend more time at the house. They played games in the evening or watched TV. They were at ease with one another, but he kept his secrets, and she didn't ask.

One evening, in the early spring, Morgan built a fire beside the barn and sat looking at the stars. He heard Veronica's footsteps and rose to meet her.

It's a beautiful night," she said, handing him a cup of coffee.

"I thought you might like it." He stirred the embers to life and the sparks danced into the obsidian sky. They sat silent, staring into the fire.

Morgan squirmed in his chair and leaned toward the fire, poking at it with a stick.

"Veronica."

She looked at him.

"Veronica, I don't have anything and I'm not going anywhere. I know how to ranch, and you need someone. We get along fine, and I do love your little girl."

"What are you trying to say, Morgan?"

"I'm trying to say, let's get married."

"Well, that's not the most romantic proposal I've ever heard but then we're not kids anymore."

"I would get down on one knee, but I still can't bend my leg. It's stiff from when the horse kicked me."

"I'm so sorry it still hurts, Morgan. Should I get down on one knee?" she asked playfully.

"Just say yes," he said.

"Yes."

Morgan pulled Veronica to her feet and kissed her, trying not to think about Sophia, lost to him somewhere across The River.

They were married at the ranch with friends of the bride attending. Carolina beamed and was happy until the day that Veronica announced that she had cancer.

Morgan pinched the bridge of his nose to stop the tears as he remembered that day. Shaking his head, he pushed himself up from the chair and stepped off the porch. He studied the house, circling the entire rock structure. It was so unlike the usual adobe or frame houses from his past. The concrete around the stones was still as tight as ever, no need to repoint again, but the windows needed to be scraped and painted. So did the trim boards. *Maybe this weekend. Monday is the showdown with the thieves. Not looking forward to that!* He went in to watch the evening news, deciding to make an early night of it.

Chapter 10
Back to Town
July 2012

Morgan awoke slowly. He was drenched in sweat from swimming, struggling to get back across The River. His arms were tired, and his neck hurt from trying to hold his head above water. Without opening his eyes, he rolled to the side of the bed, loathe to release the dream. He sat up, trying to pull his mind and body together into the same place, unhappy that he did not make it far enough to see Sophia.

He forced himself to a standing position and dressed. Aching from the exertion in his dream. *Daylight is being wasted. It's mine to do. I need to get it done.*

A pot of coffee and two dry biscuits fueled his morning and he soon headed for the barn to look for the trim paint. After checking the paint cans, he realized that he could not start the painting today. He placed a half empty can of paint in the bed of the truck and headed for the tack room.

Morgan uncovered the old Adolphus Hope saddle. Moving his hands slowly over the smooth, mahogany leather, he breathed in the dry scent of the old rigging and expertly eyed each stitch and fastener, every strap and buckle. He lifted it down, surprised at the heft of it. He had gotten so used to the modern saddles that he had forgotten how heavy the old ones were. He swung the saddle onto a frame and took down a tin of saddle soap.

Getting a bucket from its peg, he filled it with water and dampened the sponge. The astringent scent of the soap reminded him of old times. Slowly, methodically he massaged the soap into the ancient leather, exploring every nook and seam. Confident that he had cleaned every spot of the saddle, he carefully rinsed and rubbed it dry.

He then reached for the bridle and repeated the process. Soon the saddle had dried completely in the afternoon air, and he applied a coat of lanolin to each item. As he raised the saddle to its frame he inhaled deeply, enjoying the smell and feel of the old, familiar rigging. He checked the faded saddle blanket for holes and worn spots and, satisfied that it would do, rinsed it, and hung it on the rack.

Morgan was surprised that the morning had passed. His shadow ran ahead of him as he tossed a block of hay to the horses and headed toward the house.

Nursing a headache, he poured himself a glass of cold tea, made a sandwich and sought the comfort of his easy chair. He was startled awake by the sound of the ringing phone.

"Morgan, here." No answer but he heard ragged breathing. "Carolina?"

"Dad."

"What's wrong, girl?"

"It's Darren. He was here, yelling and threatening. He wants us to keep trying, but if we don't, he wants the house and his business."

"What do you want?"

"I don't know. We bought the house together. I don't think he should have it. I can't bear to think of him bringing his girlfriends to my house."

"Well Carolina. First of all, do you want to try again? You had your mind made up when you left here last week."

"Dad, I want him to change. Not run around. I don't like how I feel right now."

"Of course, you don't. Stay gathered up, Carolina. He is trying to work on you. Remember? We talked about this."

"I know, Dad, but nine years! It seems such a waste."

"How much of a waste will it be in ten years?"

"He promises to change. He says that he still loves me. He says he will make it right."

"He can do right but he can't make it right. Love proves itself, Carolina."

"What about the house?"

"Sell the house. The ranch is yours, pure and simple. You both paid for his garage. Let him keep that. He needs to make a living. Sell the house and divide any profit."

"That makes sense."

"You would have figured it out when you stop crying. I'm coming to town to get some paint and groceries. How about supper?"

"That would be great. He's moving stuff out. He'll be coming back."

"I'll be there before dark thirty."

"Bye, Dad."

Morgan stood in the shower, letting the hot water run over his aching shoulders. He bowed his head to let the pulsing water massage his neck. Twisting his head from side to side, he soaped up and washed off two days of sweat and stupidity. Finishing, he stepped back, adjusted the nozzle, and turned the hot water off, letting the cold water run over his head and down his face.

Stepping from the tub, he wiped the steam from the mirror and studied his face, shocked at how tired he looked. And old. *Things are stacking up. Lordy! I need to get shed of some of this. That girl, God bless her, has got to get a hold on things. Time is running out for me. I need to get across The River, at least once to see if I can get back to Sophia. Will she be married? Can I get back to where I was, or will I end up in another place?*

He heard the phone ring, breaking his train of thought, and ignored it. The answering machine picked up. "Hello. Mr. Donnally, you have been selected to receive..." Morgan tuned out the voice and lathered up his face. *One more thing I dislike about being in this place.*

Morgan entered the paint store with the can of paint. "May I help you, sir?"

"Yes. I need two gallons of this." Morgan set the half-empty can on the counter.

"Give me a few minutes," the clerk said, checking the color number.

Morgan wandered around the store, waiting impatiently. After paying for the paint and tucking the receipt in his pocket, he set the cans in the bed of the truck and headed for the grocery store.

Entering the store, he looked around, half-hoping to see the little boy he had encountered two days before. *I wonder what his mom looks like,* he thought idly.

Gathering a few staples, Morgan remembered that Carolina was going to be at the ranch at the end of the week and picked up some things that he knew she would like. He paid for the groceries and carried them to the truck. Placing them in the back seat, he recalled that he was out of whiskey. Heading for the liquor store at the edge of town, he was surprised to find a sign which directed him around to the side of the building. A man soon appeared and greeted him.

"What is this?" Morgan asked, indicating the boarded-up window.

"State law. Can't serve through a window. Haven't for a few years now. What can I get for you?"

"Two Seagram's, one Crown Royal," he said, gesturing a size, "and a six of Seven-Up."

The man soon appeared with the items and took the money.

Morgan arrived at Carolina's house before dark. Noticing Darren's work truck, he stepped out of his vehicle and approached the front door. Darren charged through the door carrying a suitcase and glared at Morgan as he shouldered his way to his truck.

The older man stepped aside, against his natural inclinations. Opening the front door, he called, "Carolina?"

"I'm coming."

"What's going on? Did he hurt you?"

"No, just the usual threats and denials. Let me brush my hair."

Morgan scanned the room, looking for signs of conflict. Finding none, he said, "I'll be in the truck."

Chapter 11
A Band Saw and a Brand
2012

Morgan rode silently beside Travis as they crossed his pasture. He pulled a phone from his pocket. "Tom, we're going through Travis's gate. Where are you? ... Good. Turn off the ringers on your phones. If we need to communicate, use texting. You know how to do that, right? ... You and Eldrige park up by the highway so they won't see any dust. Ride in from there. Travis and I will stay in the trees until we spot you."

They stayed horseback, silently watching for the two men.

"Here they come, Travis. It's time to dance."

Eldrige and Tom dismounted and eased up to the front door of the old rock house. Travis's horse nickered and Tom's horse responded. Tom, realizing that a change in plans was necessary, stepped quickly to the side of the old wooden door.

The door opened cautiously and soon a bare brown hand, holding a pistol, pushed through the slight opening. Tom grabbed the hand, kicked the door open and jerked the tall Mexican through the opening, slamming him to the ground. Travis quickly subdued him, holding him there with his rifle pressed against the man's throat. Morgan stepped into the room, adding his rifle to fracas. Two men were working, one at the band saw. The other was holding a large butcher knife. He slowly bent and placed the knife on the floor. The men, looking from one to the other of the men, raised their hands. Morgan switched off the compressor.

"This is quite a setup you boys have here," he said, buying time, sizing up the situation. Morgan studied the beef butchering operation. Two by eight planks were stretched across sawhorses and held the band saw and a set of knives. A wooden crate with pieces of butcher paper with a pen on top and a roll of the paper laying on the floor completed the packaging station. The saw was plugged in to the generator. A camp lantern hung from a nail, illuminating the work area. The two windows were covered with butcher paper.

"Eldrige," Morgan called. Eldrige entered and Morgan directed him to determine how many were working. A string of Spanish ensued.

Eldrige said, "They say there's only three of 'em."

"Ask the one on the ground out there. See if he says the same thing. Find out their names and where they're from."

Eldrige stepped outside and spoke to the frightened man. Returning to the house he said, "Morgan, the one outside is the leader, and his name is Calazon. That means big head." Gesturing toward the man at the saw Eldrige said, "His name is Ojon and the other one is Illorona. That's Bug-eyed and Crybaby. They are cousins and come from a place called Ojo De Santano. Doesn't sound right, but I don't think we are going to get much else out of 'em."

"Get them both outside," Morgan growled in his best effort at intimidation. He gestured towards the door with his rifle.

As the two prisoners lined up outside, Calazon tried to rise from the dirt. Travis spun his rifle around and slammed the man in the forehead, driving him back to the ground. He left a bloody gash in the man's face.

"Ask them where they get the beef and where they sell it. See if they have any ID." A flurry of Spanish filled the air as the butchers tried to explain away the pile of bones by the door and the hide rolled up in the bed of the ancient, rusty pick up.

"They say that they buy the calves from friends and sell the beef in town to people. They don't know who they are."

Tom roughly grabbed each man in turn and searched them. Finding nothing, he knelt beside the man on the ground and rolled him from one side to the other as he dug into his pockets.

"Nothing here, Morgan. Some money. They travel light."

Morgan raised his rifle until it was pointed first on one and then the others. Slowly, deliberately he scowled at the dark face and black eyes of each man, glaring at each one in turn, studying them each from head to foot, pausing until each of them understood his intention. The smallest man began to tremble and looked to make a break for The River. Eldrige lifted the butt of his rifle and with a resounding crack sent the young man to the ground. He kicked him in the ribs, encouraging him to get up. When the boy stood, there was a stain slowly spreading and darkening his pants as it made a track down his leg.

Morgan's anger surged as he thought of these men stealing what he and his friends worked so hard to accumulate. He watched the stain and imagined the kid's boot filling with urine. He studied the boy with his red cap pulled low over both ears as though he could hide inside. He remembered Weasel and the red cap pulled down around his face as he slid into the Vermillion. Morgan wondered if Weasel had been as afraid as this boy appeared to be. He gestured for the man on the ground to get up and stand beside the two.

"Let him up, Tom." Tom kicked the man as he rose to join the others.

Morgan reached into the back of the pickup and unrolled the hide. The bile rose in his throat, and he cleared it to speak.

"Looks like this one is yours, Tom," Morgan said, holding up the hide, exposing the brand.

"Sorry sons a bitches!" Tom started toward the men, red-faced and breathing hard. Lifting a ham fist, he rammed it into the face of the tall man, knocking him backward, splattering blood over both men. He followed him, driving a knee between the man's legs, causing him to drop to his knees, gagging.

"Tom! Wait! We don't want to do anything we'll have to answer for. Eldrige, you tell these boys that if any of us ever see any of them or their pickup in this county again they will be shot. Make sure they understand."

Eldrige turned and spoke to the man, pointing his finger, first at the three men and then at Morgan and Tom. He ended the tirade with, "Entiendes?"

They nodded silently, scrambled into the old, green pickup and pulled away, leaving a cloud of dust to settle over the area.

Eldrige turned around, grinning. "I told them that you and Tom were policemen and if we ever see them again, they'll be shot and thrown in The River with the bones. Apparently, they've had trouble with the law before. They'll regret this to their dying days if they live that long."

"Good thinking, Eldrige." Morgan said, smiling at his turn of phrase. "Well, we're losing daylight. It's going to take us a while to finish cutting up Tom's beef."

He stepped inside and flipped the switch on the compressor. The afternoon passed as they cut and wrapped the meat, packing it in the ice chests which had been left behind.

Chapter 12
The Day After
2012

Morgan stood at the rails of the corral, studying the roan colt. It reminded him of another young horse he had purchased long ago. Skittish, with wide-set intelligent eyes watching Morgan, the horse backed away and snorted. *He might be a little harder to work than the dun.*

Morgan shook out a loop and rolled it into the air, waiting to see which way the horse moved. After dodging the first throw, the roan changed direction and met the loop before he could dip his head and spin again. The large colt reared and pulled away, pawing the air. Morgan held on, walking hand over hand up the rope and giving the horse his head until he was in front of the frightened roan. He continued flipping the rope under the horse's chin, backing him. The colt, traveling on hind legs, stumbled and fell. Morgan held his head down, using the animal's natural fear of being vulnerable to teach him.

Allowing the horse to rise, Morgan let the rope play out and soon had him running in circles against the rails in the round corral. He stepped forward, forcing the horse to change direction and did this time and again until the two-year-old had learned his second lesson. The colt licked his lips and watched Morgan. He recognized that the roan was processing what he had learned. He walked his way up the rope, approaching slowly, speaking softly to the quivering animal, Morgan moved hand over hand until he was standing beside him.

He stood like that, not moving, until the roan turned his head slightly to study Morgan. "Well, my friend, that's enough for today." He slid the rope slowly from the sweaty neck, easing it carefully over the ears of the weary animal.

Well, a good day's work deserves a good night's rest. Morgan fed the horses and headed for the house, wondering if there was anything in the refrigerator that he wouldn't have to cook. There were cold biscuits and tomatoes on the counter and a half-finished sirloin in the refrigerator. Pouring a glass of tea and filling his plate, he aimed for his easy chair. The drone of the news commentator lulled him to sleep.

Morgan woke at daylight, surprised to find himself in bed and lay there wondering what should be first on his list of things to do. Deciding, he rose, dressed in old clothes, and fixed his standard fare of beef, eggs, and biscuits.

Breakfast concluded, he put two biscuits in his pocket and went to the corral. He fed the horses and studied the roan. Morgan stepped into the corral and let Hunter and the old dun come to him, nuzzling his shoulder. He fed them each a dry biscuit and watched the roan studying the action. Morgan ignored him. He went to the barn and gathered his painting supplies. Standing back from the house, he determined his plan. Might as *well lead the sun so that I can work in the shade.*

The morning passed as he scraped the chipped paint from the wooden frames and re-caulked every gap as he found it. Getting a taller ladder, he then scraped the soffit and fascia, sanding as he went. He worked through the heat of the day and finished as the sun burned a hole in the horizon. Walking around the house, he looked for anything he might have missed. Satisfied with what he had done, he gathered the supplies and headed for the barn. *Job well done, Lieutenant Donnally.*

Another dreamless night followed as he worked his way one step closer to being done on this side of The River.

Morning broke hot and angry. Morgan set the tea jug in the yard and scrambled three eggs to match the leftover biscuits. Washing down everything with a pot of coffee, he realized that he was just stalling. *The paint will dry too fast in this heat, that leaves the colt. The roan needs a lot of groundwork before I get on him.*

Morgan roped the gelding. The colt responded well, and Morgan began lunging him in circles, alternating directions, re-enforcing yesterday's lesson. An hour of exercise ended with a flick of the rope and Morgan snubbed the horse to a post, leaving him to learn to stand and tire him out for his next lesson.

Two glasses of iced tea on the front porch gave Morgan time to cool off and study the young horse. *I'm going to have to ease into this one. He must be fresh out of the hills. No wonder I got him so cheap. I'll have to do blanket work first.*

Morgan went to the barn and, grabbing a saddle blanket, shook it out and took it to the corral. He hung it over the top rail so the colt could see and smell it. He leaned there, upwind from the animal, so the colt could smell him.

The shadow of man and horse began to lengthen when Morgan stepped into the corral and untied the rope. The horse backed away instead of shying as he had before. *That's a good sign.*

Morgan put a halter on the roan and tied him to the fence rail. He lightly touched the large gelding and rubbed his neck, working his hand over shoulders that began to quiver. Morgan stepped away and left the horse standing in the shade of an old cottonwood which shaded one side of round pen.

Morgan spent the afternoon doing accounts and was startled when the phone rang.

"Morgan here."

"Hi, Dad. What are you doing?"

"Getting ready to start supper. Are you coming out tonight?"

"No, I have some things to tie up. I'll be out in the morning. Are you going to be around the house?"

"Yep. I'm going to start at daylight and try to finish painting. I've been working on the house. It's getting a little tired looking."

"Save me a brush. I'll be out around ten."

"Will do, girl. See you tomorrow."

"Bye, Dad," she said to a dead line.

Chapter 13
The Broken Stirrup
2012

Carolina drove up and watched her dad eyeing the sullen, bleached sky. Morgan picked up the bucket from the porch and carefully watered the lavender bushes he had planted in the spring. *Funny how he took such care of them. He never cared about flowers before. He looks tired. No, not tired. Worn. There is something more than just this ranch weighing on him. Maybe he will tell me, sometime.*

"Hi, Dad. Sorry I'm late. I got a call from the college. It was a conference call. Are you done for the day? It's getting hot."

"Yep. Can't paint in the heat. It dries too fast. Let's get some tea."

The next morning, Carolina lay awake, staring at the ceiling. She heard the front door click as her dad shut it quietly behind him. She knew that he was standing, as he did every morning, smelling the air, studying the sky. Weather was always on his mind. It frequently determined his tasks for the day.

She wondered why he stood there for so long, facing The River. *What was he thinking? Was he praying? He never said.*

She slipped out of bed and dressed quickly, gathering her long dark hair in a clasp. Maybe she could beat him to the kitchen and fix breakfast for the two of them. She could use her mom's old recipes but instead of lard she would use butter, mince some apples, and add some sugar and cinnamon. *I wonder how old the spices are. Probably back from my college days. Well, that couldn't hurt anything.*

Morgan smiled as he opened the door and saw his daughter at the kitchen sink, peeling the apples.

"Morning, Dad. Why don't you get some coffee and keep me company? I'm going to fix breakfast, for a change." Morgan poured himself a cup of coffee and, stopping behind Carolina, kissed her on the top of her head before continuing to his spot at the end of the wooden table.

He sat quietly, waiting for her to speak. She also waited and finally looked over her shoulder at him, hoping he would say something. He didn't.

"Dad, I started the paperwork for the divorce. Darren swears that it will never happen again and that he loves me and wants to work things out."

"Jeremiah 13:23." Morgan said.

"I know Dad, a leopard can't change his spots."

Morgan watched her. Carolina looked more and more like her mother. He had only been married to Veronica for... Eight? Nine years? He had grown quite fond of her, even as he came to love the little girl who had grown into the woman who stood before him now.

"It'll be nice to eat someone's cooking besides mine," he said as he shifted in his usual chair. "The older you get the more you remind me of your mother."

Carolina twisted her neck to look at him. her hands full of apples. "Dad, tell me about her. I'm losing my memories. What was she like?"

"You look like her. She was tall and broad shouldered. Dark hair like yours. She wasn't very strong. Not physically but in her heart. She came from South Carolina. That's where you got your name."

"Why didn't they go back to South Carolina?"

"She missed the South, but your dad loved this ranch and this country. She loved him but she never quite settled in. She was a southern lady. She was charming and beautiful, but she wasn't strong and independent like you."

He fell silent, thinking of Veronica.

"What else, Dad? What color were her eyes?"

"They were Turk green," he said, using the old term.

"Turk green? Do you mean turquoise?"

"Yes. turquoise. And she could look deep inside a person. You never could put anything past her. I always thought she could read my mind."

"I remember that. I was always scared not to tell her the truth. But she couldn't read your thoughts. She always wondered what you were thinking."

"Hmmm. Well, she was a good cook. I never had trouble getting help when I was working cattle because the men knew they would be well fed. She taught me a thing or two about that."

"What was her voice like?"

"I don't know. She was soft-spoken. She sounded like a grown woman. Not like a little girl. She never had to raise her voice. In fact, when she got mad, she could hardly speak. Her throat closed up, I guess. You know, she didn't have any family. When she came out here, she was all alone except for your dad. She depended on him. When she lost him, she…"

"She what, Dad?"

"She—she broke. She had you and the ranch and it was too much for her. That's why I stayed. That's why I stayed…" His voice trailed off.

Carolina, turned to look at him, and saw the pain in his face. She changed the subject. "Dad, why do you still keep jars of pickle juice in the refrigerator?"

"Because I drink it in the summer when it gets hot."

"You know they have pills for that now, don't you?"

"Yes, but I have the pickle juice and I would have to buy pills."

That seemed to settle the subject of the pickle juice. She slid the pan of fritters into the oven and got out the mound of roast to shave thin strips to drop into the hot skillet.

"Two eggs?"

"Yes."

The sound of a pickup on the gravel caused Morgan to rise and go to the front door. He waved at the woman and gestured her into the house. The sturdy blonde entered, smiling at him, and handed him two dozen eggs. "Hi, Morgan."

"Hello, Arlene. You know my daughter."

Carolina turned and greeted the woman. "I remember Arlene. How are you?"

"Right as rain, Carolina."

"And twice as welcome. Help yourself to the freezer. Do you have time for coffee?" Morgan asked.

"Sorry to show up so early but I was afraid that if I waited until later that you would be out and about somewhere. I would love some coffee."

She headed for the freezer and gathered a few packages of meat into a shopping bag.

"Morgan, thank you so much for the beef. I don't know what I would do without you."

"You would do just fine, but I am glad that we trade. I eat those eggs every day."

He handed her a cup of coffee and gestured for her to sit at the table.

"What's going on, Arlene?"

She leaned across the table and spoke to him. "Did you know about the dance at the Armory on Saturday."

"I did not. Are you going?"

"Of course. I'm hoping to get a dance out of you."

Morgan and Carolina exchanged looks. "Well, Carolina is here for a while. I think we can both go."

They discussed the local news as Carolina finished cooking and began filling the plates.

"How about some beef and eggs, Arlene?"

"No thanks. Gotta go. See you Saturday."

As Morgan and Carolina ate, they discussed ranch matters and the upcoming dance. Soon they were finished and went to get the paint supplies. Carolina painted the window trim and Morgan climbed the taller ladder to paint the soffit and fascia. Skipping the noon meal, they were finished in the early afternoon.

Carolina awoke and listened for the sounds of morning. She could hear birds chirping outside but the radio was not on in the kitchen. She could not hear her dad. *He must be sleeping in, or sick.* She jumped out of bed, concerned. The pain in her shoulders and arms stopped her. Radiating fire ran up her arms and her shoulders, meeting in a large knot at the base of her neck. Slipping on her robe and slippers, she eased her way into her dad's room and looked around. The bed was made.

"Dad?" She called as she scuffed hurriedly into the kitchen.

No answer. She stuck her head out the back door and looked around. "Dad?"

Still no answer. She stepped gingerly on to the porch and down the steps. The faint drum of hooves drew her around the side of the barn where she found her father, eyes focused on the roan, watching every move, every twitch of the ear, every turn of the head, learning the colt.

Carolina stood with her robe wrapped tightly around her, watching them until Morgan noticed her and waved. She waved back and returned to the house. He had left a plate of scrambled eggs, covered, on the counter. *He is one tough old bird. Here I am crippling around, and he is up and at 'em as usual. He reminds me of black coffee, barb wire, and latigo,* she thought, shaking her head.

Back at the house, she poured water into the reservoir of the coffee pot. When it was ready, she poured the coffee in to her special mug. She thought about her dad, heating milk to pour with a little coffee in that same mug. They would take their coffee and sit on the front porch to watch the sun come up. A favorite memory.

She ate and was sitting with a second cup of coffee when the phone rang.

"Donnally residence."

"Well! I wasn't expecting you. How are you doing, girl?"

With an intake of breath Carolina said, "Hello, Travis." The words caught in her throat.

"I'm fine, how are you and the girls?" she asked.

The sound of his voice still sent rivers of emotion coursing through her.

"All's well on the home front. What are you doing out here?"

"I'm here for the summer."

"Really? We should get together and catch up. Is Darren with you?"

"No. I told Darren that I want a divorce. I'm just here to decompress."

"I'm sorry to hear that, Carolina. It must be hard. Is your dad around?"

"He's out working a horse. Do you want me to get him?"

"No. That's okay. I'll catch him later. Thanks."

She slowly hung up the phone as if she could hold on to the connection, and Travis. She turned her attention to the calendar hanging on the wall. It was still turned to May. Lifting the page to June, she studied the picture of running horses above the insurance advertisement as she hooked the page to the nail. A doodle in the corner of the sixteenth of June caught her attention and she studied it. It was not like her dad to draw. He seldom spent enough time on the phone to pick up a pen. The tree was sparse, like a poplar or lodge pole pine. There was one broken branch lying on the ground against the trunk.

Carolina stood there pondering the meaning. Suddenly it hit her, the realization punching her in the chest. She gasped, sucking in air that felt like knives. Tears started down her cheeks, unbidden.

She remembered and grieved that day. She did not know that her dad remembered. They never talked about it. The anniversary of the day she lost the baby. This was the real reason that she had married Darren. *A stupid college fling. Created by loneliness and fueled by alcohol.*

She bent over the kitchen sink and threw cold water on her face. Getting dressed, she grabbed her keys and left the house, heading to the far north pasture. Her safe place when she needed to be alone and think.

Opening and closing two gates, she came to the lake, surrounded by Afghan, juniper and cottonwoods. The wildflowers were still blooming. Soon they would wilt and dry up from the heat. Summer always came before the calendar said it would. At least summer held its coolness around the lake. Parking the truck, she walked to the water's edge and stood, watching the sunlight dance on the water.

Trout broke the surface, leaving small radiating circles. She stood there watching, waiting for the trout to leap. The joyousness of their play stood in sharp contrast to her mood. Picking up a rock, she threw it into the lake. The small discharge of energy caused her to pick up another stone and fling it harder into the water. Feeling the release, she reached down and gathered a handful of rocks. Throwing them one at a time, she watched the concentric rings move toward shore. The anger and grief rose in her and she matched it by flinging the rocks farther and harder until she was grunting with the effort. Faster and harder she threw, brushing tears roughly from her face. Deep, wracking sobs wrenched the pain through her consciousness.

She looked around for a place to sit and started for the stand of trees. Deer droppings left a trail, which she followed as she made her way through the grove. She stopped and looked up when she heard the barking of the red-tailed squirrels warning each other of her presence. Yip. Yip. Yip. She sat still and could hear the leaves murmuring. She cried silently until her tears tasted like rain. Leaning against a tree, Carolina sat.

Morgan waited until late in the evening to call his daughter. "Where did you go, Carolina? I was getting concerned."

"I'm sorry I didn't tell you, Dad. Something came up. I just needed to be alone. I think I'll go visit Lizbeth. Do you remember her? We were in college together. I need to get away from everything for a few days. I should be back for the dance on Saturday."

"Take care, sweetheart. If you need me, let me know."

"I will, Dad."

He knew when she needed him, and she knew that he would not pry. He always told her that it's one thing to care but another thing to meddle.

Morgan was up before the sun. This day he would start with the saddle work. He studied the well-thumbed Farmer's Almanac as he ate his morning eggs.

Lifting the saddle from its frame, he carried it to the corral and set it on the top rail. The colt slowly approached the new element. Morgan let him sniff and inspect the saddle. When the roan lost interest, Morgan took his rope off the post and eased up to the horse. The roan turned to face him, wary but unflinching. Morgan eased the loop over the colt's head, being cautious with his ears. The horse began running in circles with little encouragement. Morgan worked him until he was warmed up.

He snubbed the colt to a post and eased the saddle and blanket on to the sweaty back. The horse attempted to rear and fling his head. Unable to get away, he stood quivering as Morgan again eased the saddle to his back. Again, the fight, again the saddle lifted to his back. Over and over, until the horse stood for the saddle. Morgan untied the rope and began walking the horse in circles. He then urged the horse into a trot. As the saddle bounced on the back of the animal, the stirrups began to flap. The bucking which ensued was an attempt to dislodge the saddle. Once again, snubbed, then lunged. Over and over until the bucking stopped. Morgan then snubbed the horse and cinched the saddle. This action started another round of lunging and bucking. Failing to dislodge the saddle by pitching, the colt laid down and rolled. Morgan stepped close and twisted the animal's head around, keeping the horse from rising. *I'm glad this is not my good saddle. He sure is hard on my gear.*

Once the roan lay still, Morgan let him up and flicked the rope, making the horse trot in circles, getting used to the feel of the saddle moving on his back. Morgan frowned with an oncoming headache and stopped the circling animal. He unsaddled and released him. Leaving the saddle on the railing, he returned to the house. Tea, aspirin and a nap ensued.

Late in the afternoon, Morgan took a bridle out to corral. Roping the colt, he began introducing him to the bridle. He rubbed the reins over his neck until the horse stood. Slowly, speaking softly, he eased the bit into the animal's mouth and eased the head strap over the ears. Buckling the cheek strap, he led the horse around until the animal complied with directions. Morgan then took his rope and tied it to each side of the bridle and got behind the colt. He drove him, pulling the head to turn first in one direction and then the other.

"Well, that's enough for the day, fella. We will try something else tomorrow."

The horse did not respond.

Morgan woke with a sense of dread, realizing that this was the day. He would mount the horse. Not enough schooling had been done but he really needed to get that horse rode. He needed to get some miles on him before he tried to cross The River. He bridled and saddled the roan and put him on the lunge line. *Might as well sap him out a little before I go topside.*

Morgan brought the horse to a standstill and stepped one foot into the stirrup, shifting his weight to the animal. The colt spread his legs, adjusting to the new burden. Morgan gingerly eased into saddle. *So far, so good.* They stood like that, not moving until Morgan gently touched the sides of the colt with his heels.

Without an outward sign, the roan exploded. kicking his heels high, bowing his back, bucking. Morgan held on to the saddle horn with one hand, raising the reins with the other, pulling the colt's head upward. The horse did not submit but began to pitch unpredictably, launching himself high and coming down with a tooth-rattling, spine-jarring pounding to the ground. Morgan held on, unable to do anything else. Suddenly, the horse ran at the planks of the corral and tried to jump, breaking the top rail. Morgan heard the crack as the rail gave way and felt a sharp, brutal pain in his right leg.

"Son..of..a..bitch!" He slipped from the horse as the animal backed away from the broken timber. "Damn it to hell and back!" Morgan lay in the dirt, waiting for the first wave of pain to wash through him. *Now what?* He studied the roan and the roan looked back. "I guess we are at a standoff for now, butthead. The fat's in the fire."

Morgan reached for his hat and slid under the bottom rail. He felt for his keys. *Damn it.* He pulled himself laboriously to his feet, holding on to the fence post, then turned and hopped, dragging the damaged leg. Morgan reached the kitchen door and stood holding on to the door frame, catching his breath. He reached inside and felt for his keys and phone. He tapped number one. *No answer. Of course, she said that she was leaving town.* He tapped number two. After several rings Travis picked up. "Travis here."

"Travis. Morgan. I'm headed to town. I broke my leg working the colt."

"I'll come and get you."

"No. It would be quicker to just meet me in town. Call ahead for me. I don't know how this will play out."

"Will do. Meet you at the hospital."

"Thanks."

Morgan grabbed a kitchen chair and used it as a walker to make his way to the pickup. Laboriously he pulled himself in to the Dodge on the passenger side and slid across the seat. He tucked his left foot under his right leg to reach the pedal. Sitting sideways under the wheel, he started for Dickson.

The doctor entered Morgan's room. "Well Morgan, that was quite a fracture, The X-rays showed a new trauma along the lines of an old injury. What happened?"

Morgan, unwilling to share said, "Don't remember Doc. What are you going to do?"

I have ordered a painkiller. You may sleep for a while. It is going to take some time to get you cleaned up and prepped for a cast."

Travis entered behind the nurse. "Damn, Morgan! You look like nine miles of bad road!"

"I feel like it," he said briefly, embarrassed by his plight. He rolled over, allowing the nurse to inject the pain killer in his hip.

"I was working the colt. He got the better of me. Tore up the round corral. He's still saddled. This is going to take a while, Travis. Can you take care of him?"

"What do you want me to do, shoot him?" he asked, grinning.

"No. Not yet. Just unsaddle and feed him and turn out the others. Feed Jake and bring me another pair of pants. Doc tore up these. Might as well bring me a set of clothes. You might need to buy me something that will fit over the cast."

"I'll take care of everything. Be back later. Did you get hold of Carolina?"

"No. She's out of pocket."

"Good enough. I'll be back."

Morgan nodded. The medicine was kicking in and he didn't care much one way or the other.

He woke to the familiar pain of a broken leg. Travis was seated beside him, thumbing through a magazine. "Well, pardner, how do you feel?"

Morgan shook his head.

"Tell you what. Why don't you come home with me for a few days? I can take care of the horses and Jake."

"Thanks, but I think I'm going to go home. Carolina left word that she would be here tomorrow. If you can get me home, she can pick up my truck later."

"That works. Are you ready to go?" Travis asked, eyeing the hospital gown.

"As soon as I get out of this cutty-sark," he said, reaching back to untie the gown.

"The what?" Travis frowned at the strange words from his neighbor.

Morgan pulled at the edges of the gown to indicate what he meant. "I'll be ready in a minute."

"You have to sign out."

"I guess they'll know I'm gone when the bed's empty."

Travis laughed. "That's not the way it works, Morgan. I'll be right back."

He returned, trailing a nurse with a clipboard.

Travis followed Morgan into the house, setting the medicines on the kitchen table. "I'll fix you something to eat, Morgan," Travis said, reaching into the refrigerator. He pulled out the cooked roast and began slicing it. "How many sandwiches?" he called from the kitchen.

"Two. I haven't eaten since yesterday. Make yourself something."

"What do you want to drink?"

"There's whiskey in the cupboard."

Travis poured two stiff drinks and juggled them and the sandwiches to the living room.

"I don't think you're supposed to mix the meds with booze so take it easy. So! What really happened out there?" Travis handed him the drink.

"That colt is tough and knows lots of tricks. He's smart. He has some scars. I think someone tried to break him before."

"That's probably why he was in the horse sale," Travis volunteered.

"Right. I got in a hurry. Not enough groundwork." He ducked his head, embarrassed that the colt had bested him.

"You also blew a stirrup. No wonder you couldn't stay on board. Want me to sap him out?"

Morgan thought about it and then said, "No, I really need to do this myself."

"Okay. I have to go pick up the girls. Do you need anything for now?"

"No. I'm going to sit here for a while and then go to bed."

"Here's your crutch. I'll check on you in the morning."

"Thanks, Travis."

Morgan heard the sound of Carolina's truck. She entered and saw Morgan in sweatpants, seated in his easy chair.

"Dad! What happened?"

"Well, I've heard that good judgment comes with experience and experience comes from poor judgment. I got some experience yesterday."

"That doesn't sound like you, Dad."

"I got in a hurry. I need you to bring my truck back. It's at the hospital."

"I'll call Travis, he can take me in."

"I'm sure that'll be fine. He should be here soon."

"I'll fix you breakfast."

"I sure would like a cup of coffee."

"I'm on it."

"Are you saving this clabbered milk for biscuits, Dad?" she called from the kitchen.

"Yes."

Travis showed up with his younger girl in tow. "Morning, Carolina. You remember Carly?"

Carolina said to the child, "Yes I do. What a cutey you are." The child said nothing as she stared up at Carolina.

Travis went to the living room and spoke to Morgan. Returning to the kitchen he said. "Well. The first order of business is to go get his truck. I'll go feed while you finish with his breakfast. Does that work for you?" Carolina nodded, without answering.

With the child buckled in the back seat, Travis began to speak. "I was sorry to hear about you and Darren. I hope things are going to be okay. Do you have any plans?"

"No. I'm going to stay at the ranch until school starts." She studied his profile and struggled for something to say. *I grew up with this man. We've been neighbors all our lives. Rode the same school bus. He was the first man to make love to me. It shouldn't be this hard to talk to him.*

"Travis, can we talk?"

He glanced at the back seat. "Not now."

She could feel the anger and hurt rise up in him. His jaw tightened. He said nothing. They rode in silence until they reached the hospital and Carolina stepped out of the truck.

"Thanks for the ride."

"You're welcome. Morgan is going to need help around the place. I'll be over every morning for a while. Call me if you need anything, Carolina. I mean that."

"Thank you."

Morgan sat in his easy chair with his right foot propped on the ottoman. Thoughts ran in a tumble through his mind. *Damn. Damn. Damn.*

He felt the clock of his life ticking away and doubled his fists, pounding on the arms of the chair.

The next morning, Travis appeared at the back door and tapped lightly before letting himself in. Finding Carolina in the kitchen he said, "Morning, Sunshine. How is our patient this morning?"

"Getting crankier by the minute."

Travis found Morgan in the office, drinking coffee, staring out of the window.

"Hello, partner. Doing any better?"

"Some. Don't like this one bit."

"I'm not surprised. What do you need done today? I don't have Carly with me. Mom has her for the day."

"Travis, I really need to check the waters and the east fence in the north pasture. I put in a new one three years ago and every time the wind blows the sand banks up. If it gets too high the cows will walk over it."

"I'll take care of it, boss," Travis said, touching the brim of his hat.

"Why don't you have Carolina pack a basket and make a day of it. I know she's getting very tired of me. I'm getting tired of me."

Travis saluted and turned on his heel, returning to the kitchen.

"Carolina, your dad suggested that we pack a lunch and go check the waters and the north pasture fence." She turned around to look into his eyes, trying to read meaning in his words.

"I'll feed while you finish up here. That work for you?"

"I'll be ready when you are, Travis." Her voice cracked.

Seated in the truck, she leaned against the door and studied his profile. The copper curls lay against his neck, curving over the collar of his white shirt.

When he turned to speak to her, the amber eyes that could turn so dark when he was angry flashed at her, going over her body quickly before returning to her face.

"We might as well get this out in the open, Carolina. I thought we had an understanding. We had a plan. When we finished school, we would get married and stay on the ranch."

"That was the plan. I'm so sorry for the way things turned out, Travis. I could hardly stand to be away from you and the ranch. I was very lonely."

"So was I," he said, coldly.

"In all fairness, Travis, you were chasing around when we were in high school."

"I don't deny that, but when we left for college, I thought we understood each other."

"We did," she said, fighting back tears. She watched a muscle rope along his jawline as he returned his eyes to the dusty road.

When they got to the first gate he moved to step from behind the wheel.

"I'll get it," she said stepping down from the truck.

He studied her as she pulled the gate aside and waited for him to drive through.

"What happened that you couldn't wait?' he continued when she returned to the truck.

"It was stupid. I was so lonely one night and I tried to call you. Your room-mate said that you were at a roping and wouldn't be back that night. I went to a party and Darren was there. We knew each other from school and just started talking and drinking. One thing led to another."

"It led to you getting pregnant, that's where it led." He spit the words at her. "Why didn't you tell me, Carolina? I would've married you."

"You say that now, but who knows what you would have done."

"No one knows anything for sure," he admitted.

Travis stopped and stepped out of the truck. He reached in the back and pulled out a shovel.

Carolina trailed behind him, staring at his rigid back.

"Travis, could we put this behind us and start out again, as friends?"

Travis stabbed sharply at the tumbleweeds banked against the barbed wire fence. Breaking them into smaller pieces, he tossed them over the wire.

"That's all we can do. I have two little girls and they come first."

The glimmer of hope that she carried vaporized with his words.

"I understand. Shall we stop and eat?"

"I need to check the tanks first," he said sharply, avoiding her eyes.

Silence fell between them as they fought to control fiery emotions.

They traveled in silence while the water tanks were inspected. Travis spotted a stand of trees and drove to them. Getting out, he pulled a blanket from the back seat and lifted the basket out. He shook out the blanket with rocking horses on it and spread it on the ground.

She stood in front of him. "Travis?" He squinted, studying her face. She moved slightly so that he was facing the sun, preventing him from looking deeply into her eyes. He reached up and pulled his hat down to shade his face. He held his ground, playing the dance they were engaged in. She didn't want him to read her eyes, to know the emotions that he had awakened. He didn't want her to see the hunger in his.

"Let's eat," he said.

Carolina settled herself and reached in the basket for two Mason jars full of tea. Holding them up, she said, with forced cheerfulness, "If we broke one, I didn't want it to be one of Dad's good glasses."

"Good thinking."

She handed him a sandwich and they both leaned back against the tree, studying the landscape. Silence filled the space between them as they ate. Travis broke the muteness and said with forced cheerfulness, "During my summers I would hire out away from the ranch. I thought that I would be more independent and find something other than ranching. This sandwich reminds me of why I never liked farming.

"Why is that?"

"Because farmers expect you to bring your own lunch. Ranchers feed you."

"So true." She laughed.

"Your dad has done a good job of bringing the grass back. He's rotating the pastures. Giving the grass a chance to rest."

"Yes, we split two of the pastures so we could let one lay out and reseed. He's been burning the brush and creosote bushes. He says that the mesquite has enough beans every year to count as a light crop," Carolina said, lightly.

"We've talked about that. I've been working on that at our ranch. Dad never would do it but when he died, I convinced Mom to try it."

"How is your mom?"

"She's wearing out. I try to keep the work load off her."

"Like my dad."

"Yep. We better head back. Callie will be getting out of school."

A new dawn, and Morgan hobbled to the table and sat watching Carolina fix breakfast.

"Carolina, this is Saturday and I want you to go to the dance. You don't need to stay here with me."

"But Dad, I really don't want to go."

"Go anyway."

Chapter 14
The Armory Dance
2012

As Carolina approached the old Armory, she saw that several of the pick-ups in the parking lot had coolers in the back. *Probably beer. Or the hard stuff.*

As she entered and held her hand to be stamped, she studied the crowd. So many faces that she didn't know. Arlene approached her and looking out the door said, "Hi, Carolina. Where's your dad?"

"He broke his leg. He won't be coming."

"What?! What happened?"

"He was breaking a horse and they broke the top rail of the pen."

"I'll have to go out there. Take him some food or something."

"Thanks, Arlene, but we have it covered. I'm staying there."

"Well, I'll still go, maybe he needs company."

"Maybe he does. See you later."

Carolina purchased a canned drink at the concession set up in the corner and found a seat at an empty table. From behind her she heard, "Why, hel-looooo good lookin'. How're you doin'?"

She spun around to find the owner of the voice. Mark Setter had squatted down so that when she turned, they were face to face. "Hello, Mark. Where's your wife?"

He grinned crookedly and said, "She's home with the kids. How about a dance?"

"No thanks. I'm just here to listen to the music."

"I heerd you 'n' Darren are broke up. Why not give ole Mark a try?"

"Mark, get out of here or I'll have to call somebody."

The man struggled to his feet and said over his shoulder, "Jus' 'member ole Mark if you get lonesome, beautiful."

An old man wobbled his way toward Carolina. She watched as he approached, a lopsided grin plastered on his wrinkled face.

"'Lo, Miz Car'lina. Can I hev this dance?" He tipped his hat.

"Certainly, Mr. Rutherford."

She stood and let him lead her to the dance floor. Holding her politely, he leaned back and gazed bleary eyed into her face. "You are bee uu tiful, Miz Car'lina."

"Thank you, Mr. Rutherford. How is your family?"

"Fine. Jes' fine, ma'am. They's here."

"I'm glad that they are, Mr. Rutherford. Thank you for the dance."

He led her to her chair and asked, "Can I hev 'nother one?"

"Maybe later. Not now."

The old man removed his hat in an exaggerated bow and tripped as he spun to go.

Carolina finished her drink and stood to find a trash can. A large, dark man appeared at her side. His shiny, black hair fell across his shoulders. In a deeply resonating voice he asked, "Have this dance?"

"Certainly," she said, holding up a hand. "How are you?"

"I'm fine." He reached for her hand and pulled her to him. She pushed slightly, indicating how close she would dance.

"My name's Donald. I'm from the Mescalero Res."

"Oh. Do you work around here, Donald?"

"No."

The dance over, she released his hand. He clasped her wrist and said, "I want another one."

She nodded and they danced one more time. Instead of returning to her table, he held her wrist and led her to a group of single men standing against a wall. He stood in front of her with his arms crossed.

She stood for a moment, surprised at this development. She slowly stepped backward and edged her way around the crowd to her table, breathing a sigh of relief.

Carolina avoided Donald's stare by directing her attention to the door. She watched Travis, with his arms full of blankets, guiding his girls through the stamping process at the entrance. He saw her and nudged the girls in that direction.

"I'm glad that you came, Carolina. I thought you wouldn't since Morgan is laid up."

"He insisted."

He spread the blankets under the table, making a bed for the girls.

"Which little girl wants to dance? Which one should I choose?" Travis teased, covering his eyes.

"Pick me! Pick me!" they squealed in unison.

"I pick, eeny, meany, miney, mo. I pick Callie. Carly, you stay here with Miss Carolina."

She watched as he swung the little girl in exaggerated circles until she giggled with delight. Carly knelt in the chair in front of Carolina and held up a hand.

"I'm this many."

"That's a lot."

"My Daddy says he knew you when you were this many," Carly said, holding up five fingers.

"He did. We even rode the school bus together."

"I don't ride the bus. Daddy takes Callie to school. I go with them."

"That's very nice, Carly."

"I can say my ABCs. Do you want me to tell them?"

"Of course, I do."

The child began to sing the alphabet song and was finishing as Travis approached with a laughing Callie slung over his shoulder.

"Okay, Carly. One dance for you, little muffin."

Returning with Carly he said, "Okay, girls. Let's get dressed for bed." Carolina watched as Travis led the girls by the hand. Each child carried her stuffed animal with pajamas inside.

Reappearing with the girls, he gently laid them down and, with his head leaning against the table, recounted a favorite bedtime story before pulling a light blanket to their shoulders. The sound of the country music made an odd background for his tale of a sleeping princess.

Carolina watched, with envy, the tenderness that Travis showed his girls. She was lost in thought, staring past the children when a hand appeared before her face.

"May I have this dance?"

She looked up to see Travis looking intently at her.

"I would love to," she said.

He led her to the dance floor and gathered her into his arms. The familiar warmth of him, the scent of him, the touch of him filled her senses. She struggled to concentrate. To follow his steps. She remembered. It felt so right to be in his arms again.

The dance ended and she choked out, "We should do this again."

He spoke softly into her ear, "We haven't finished with this time." He held her until the music started and they danced again. And again.

The lights came up and people began to leave the Armory. Travis uncovered the girls.

"I'll fold the blankets."

"Thanks," Travis said as he lifted the girls and settled them on his chest.

Carolina followed the little family to the parking lot and waited while Travis beeped the truck to unlock the doors. She held out her arms for Carly and Travis deposited Callie in her car seat. Carolina handed the blankets to him, and he stashed them on the floorboard. Following him around the end of the truck, she handed Carly to her father and opened the door. She stood watching while he settled the sleeping child into her seat. He quietly closed the door.

Travis turned around and said, "Thanks, I had a good time. So did the girls."

"I did, too."

He reached out and drew her to him, kissing her gently. Stepping back, he looked long at her and said, "Good night, Carolina." He climbed into his truck, and quietly closed the door.

"Good night," she whispered.

Chapter 15
Working Eldrige's Cattle
2012

Morgan limped to the table, using his crutch. Carolina put a plate of meat and beans in front of him.

"I made cornbread for a change, Dad. How about some jalapenos and onions?"

"Always. Looks good," he said, eyeing the plate. "It sure has been nice having you around, sweetheart."

"Me, too. We're very fortunate that I had already planned to be out here. You would have been okay, but I'm glad that I could be here to help."

"You've been a big help. Eldrige called and said that he's going to work cattle tomorrow. I want to go, even though I can't do anything. Do you want to take me and help? I still can't drive."

"Okay. I'll fix some enchiladas to take."

"Sounds good. We need to be over there by seven. They should be penning the cattle by then."

Morgan backed up to the rear seat and lifted himself into the truck. He slid across the width of the vehicle and positioned his right leg on the seat.

"Dad, do you have your pain med?"

"I don't need it."

"So, what do you always tell me? It's better to have it and not need it than need it and not have it. I'll be right back."

Returning to the pickup, she climbed behind the wheel and handed Morgan the bottle of pills. "Where are we going, Dad?"

"Out to the highway, turn north. About fourteen miles and you'll see a blue silo. Turn east and follow the right fork."

Morgan propped himself awkwardly against the door behind Carolina, with the cast encased right leg stretched out in front of him. Peering over the front seat, he directed Carolina and watched the pastureland go by. The farms, broken into fields of alfalfa, stood in green contrast to the grasslands surrounding them. The grackles swooped in black masses, like a matador's cape, from one irrigated field to another.

"There's the silo, Carolina. Turn right and then take the right fork."

"It's been a long time since I've seen Eldrige and his family. Probably since before I went to college."

"They haven't changed much. They live a little differently than we do. Eldrige helps the rest of us so we all neighbor when we need to. None of us could get the cattle worked if we didn't all pitch in."

"I remember before I left home when I would go with you and help. It was always fun. Will Travis be there?"

"Yes, and Tom. We won't get finished today."

As they approached the house, Carolina noted that bed springs on the roof were attached to a cable running in through a window. Worn out furniture sat on the front porch and farm equipment in various stages of repair along with children's toys were strewn around the yard. The adobe house appeared to be melting into the ground.

"What are the bed springs for, Dad?"

"The springs are the antenna for the television."

"Oh my," said Carolina.

"Yes. That's what I meant."

Carolina pulled up in front of the worn, old house. "Let me run this food in and then we can go to the corrals." She carried the dish into the house, making a detour around an old iron bed frame located close to the front door. The dirt inside the frame had been dug up. Flowers burst over the metal frame, filling the area with a riot of colors.

Returning to the truck, Carolina said, "What an odd thing, those flowers and that old bed."

"Mona was gone to visit her sister for a week, and she told Eldrige that she wanted a flower bed. He had this ready to surprise her when she got back."

"Boy oh boy! I bet that was a surprise."

"Yep. You have to be very specific when you talk to Eldrige. He has flights of fancy."

"What did Mona say?"

"She told him that it was a lovely flower bed. Just what she wanted."

"They sure are a funny couple, aren't they Dad?"

"They're a pair to draw to, that's for sure."

"Go ahead and pull up in front of that pickup with the trailer. We'll form an alley to funnel the cattle into the pens."

Carolina deftly parked the truck and went around to open the door for her dad.

Morgan inched himself out and onto the ground, holding on to the door as he reached for his crutch. Mona spied them. "Hi, Morgan. It's so good to see you. How're you doing?"

"I'm doing just fine, Mona." Morgan turned and gestured to his daughter. "Mona, do you remember my daughter, Carolina?"

"Of course, I do. Haven't seen you in a long time, Carolina."

"I've been away. Nice to see you. What can I do to help?"

"Get the cooler of vaccine from the back seat."

A young man, dressed in tennis shoes, an AC/DC shirt, shorts, and an oversized, black cowboy hat approached.

"Morgan, Carolina, this is Allen. He's the son of a friend of mine, Clara. He and his little brother are visiting their Aunt Eda. They're from Chicago."

"Nice to meet you, Allen. Your little brother wouldn't be Phillip, would he?"

"Yeah, that's him. What'd he do?"

"Nothing. I just met him the other day in town."

Mona turned to Allen and said, "Look lively, everyone. Here they come. Get behind the truck, Allen. They shouldn't see us."

In a cloud of dust, the herd veered away from the trucks and funneled into the corral. Mona jumped up and quickly shut and latched the gate behind them. She checked to make sure the branding irons were hot while Carolina filled syringes with vaccine. They stood ready for the men to rope and drag the calves.

"What can I do, Mona?" Allen asked.

"You can make sure that the syringes stay full. Carolina will show you how to do it."

Carolina watched Travis working the cattle. *Poetry in motion*, she thought as he threw a slow loop that settled at a calf's heels, curling around to the front of the back feet. A quick jerk tightened the coil when the calf stepped into it. He dallied and dragged the calf to the fire. The horse leaned back, digging his feet into the ground, holding the rope tight. Eldrige grabbed the rope and sat on the calf. Travis touched spurs to his mount and the horse moved forward, putting enough slack in the rope that it could be removed. Eldrige continued holding the calf down while Carl, another volunteer, cut off the necessary parts and Mona rushed in with the hot irons. The hiss and smell of burning hair filled the air as Carolina rushed forward to vaccinate the bawling calf. Allen faithfully filled the syringes and watched in fascination as the work progressed, occasionally forgetting to get out of the way.

Allen leaped to get out of the way of a drag rope and ran into Carolina. The syringe needle pricked Allen's hand.

"Help! Morgan! I've been stabbed!" Allen jumped through the rails and hurried to Morgan, holding one hand with the other. "I got stabbed with the needle! What'll I do? What'll I do?" the teen asked, bouncing up and down.

Morgan placed a large, steady hand on the boy's shoulder and held him firmly, examining the speck of blood on the boy's outstretched hand.

Looking somberly into the boy's eyes Morgan said, "Allen, it looks fine to me but," he paused, then said, "if you wake up tomorrow and crave hay, you better see a doctor." The teen looked around, puzzled at the laughter.

Mona yelled, "Let's eat."

Everyone trailed to the house and angled towards the outside faucet in the yard. A large, wooden, electric cable spool sat beside it with a bar of soap and a well-used towel on top.

Having cleaned up, they all gathered around the kitchen table laden with roast, potatoes, beans, enchiladas, and pies. A jar of pickles substituted for a vegetable. Silence settled on the group as Eldrige bowed his head and said, "Lord, thank you for this food and the hands that cooked it. We sure could use some rain if you can spare it. From ghosties and ghoulies and long-legged beasties and things that go bump in the night, please Lord deliver us. Amen."

Carolina looked sideways at Morgan. He winked at her.

Everyone filled a plate and went to the front yard, finding places on stumps and the worn sofa and chairs on the porch. Separate conversations could be heard throughout the yard.

Eldrige spoke in a subdued tone until he became engrossed in Tom's tale.

"Well, I'll be a son of a...."

"Eldrige," Mona cautioned.

"Biscuit eater," Eldrige finished lamely.

"Eldrige. We have company," Mona chided.

"Sorry." Eldrige lowered his voice and continued talking to Tom. As he got caught up in telling the next story, his voice rose, and everyone turned to look at him.

"... and her ass was as wide as an ax handle..."

"Eldrige!" Mona yelled at him.

Clara huffed, "Well I never!"

Eldrige twisted his neck around and said to her, "No ma'am, I reckon you haven't."

"Eldrige!" Mona exclaimed.

Clara stood and said, "Allen, Phillip. We are leaving. Eda, will you take us home, please?"

Mona stood, glaring at Eldrige and said, "Eda, Clara, please don't go. He doesn't know what he's saying sometimes."

Silently, the small group moved to go. The tight-lipped woman, trailed by the two boys, exited the house. Eda shrugged, "I'm sorry, Mona. Thanks for the meal. It was good."

The men stood and said goodbye.

Eldrige sat silent, listening as the men began conversations and laughed at each other's stories. Mona began clearing the dishes, moving among the men, visibly annoyed.

Eldrige, his remorse no longer evident, said, "Tom, do you remember when it rained so hard three years ago?"

"I do, Eldrige. What happened?" said Tom, feeding him straight lines.

"Well, I decided I'd raise alligators."

"I didn't know that, Eldrige. I could've used a new pair of boots. How did that work out for you?"

"I couldn't get anyone to come out here and buy them. I had a terrible time rounding them up and getting them loaded in the trailer. I took them down by the Flick a Flea Motel out on the Highway. I put up a 'For Sale, Alligators' sign but nobody stopped."

"What'd you do with them, Eldrige?"

"I finally just turned them loose."

"You turned them loose! What happened to them?"

"Last I saw them, they was headed for The River."

He waited until the laughter subsided and said, "Tom, do you know what a horse is?"

"I think I do, Eldrige, but why don't you tell me."

"Well, a horse is a full action figure. Just like those kids toys they advertise. He bites in the front and kicks in the rear and bucks in the middle." Eldrige slapped his leg and guffawed at his own joke.

As the laughter died down, Morgan rose and said, "We better get back to work."

"Do you know even one true thing, Eldrige?" asked Tom, laughing and shaking his head.

"Can't say as I do, Tom. I do try to improve the truth some." Eldrige grinned.

Carolina fell in step with her dad and said, "Wow."

Morgan nodded and said, "We do this to help Mona. She must get very tired, being out here alone with him all day, every day."

The horses were loaded, and the cattle turned out. The men shook hands and said their goodbyes. Carolina drove to the house to pick up her dish. Eldrige and Mona stood on the porch and waved goodbye.

"Ya a ta hey."

"Ya a ta hey to you, Eldrige," Morgan replied.

As they drove off, Carolina asked, "What does that mean?"

"It's a Navajo saying. It means all is good. It's something like a general greeting. At least that's how he uses it."

"Is he Navajo?"

"I don't know. It would explain some things."

"Like what?"

"Well, if you start a conversation with him, he will squat down and pull out a cigarette. Once he has it lit, he's there for the duration."

"He sure does like to talk, that's for sure."

"He can talk all afternoon. You have to keep walking backwards to get away from him or keep him working. He will finally get up and follow. We'll work the rest of the cattle tomorrow. Do you want to help?"

"Of course. I wouldn't quit in the middle of a job. You taught me better than that, Dad. It's not the cowboy way."

Chapter 16
The Discussion
2012

Carolina was unpacking a suitcase when her phone rang. "Hello, Darren," she said in a voice tight with anger.

"Hello, Carolina. How are you doing?"

"I'm doing just fine. Why are you calling?"

"I know that we're in a mess. I'm sorry for calling you names. I was just mad."

"What do you want, Darren?"

"I want to talk to you, Babe."

She cringed at that. *How dare he!* "About what?" she asked curtly.

"About us, Carolina. Nine years is a lot of time not to talk about."

"We are done talking, Darren."

"Carolina, don't be so hard. That's not like you. How about dinner or a drink or something? Let's talk a little. Please. That can't hurt, can it?"

He always appeals to my higher nature. He knows how to work me. Nine years is a lot to toss out.

"A drink," she said, reluctantly.

"How about the No Name around seven tonight? It's Tuesday so there won't be a crowd," he offered.

"I'll be there."

Carolina pulled open the heavy, red metal door and stepped into the dim, paneled interior. The stench of stale beer and old cigarettes assaulted her. She looked around and the bartender nodded a greeting. The brass footrail shone in the dim light and the mirror behind the bar reflected the room's tired interior. Wall sconces threw faint circles of light over the worn oak dance floor and stained carpet. She could see an older woman mopping the bathroom floor and the urine smell, mixed with the disinfectant, assailed her senses. Gesturing to a booth in the corner, the bartender asked her what she would have.

"Crown and Seven, please," she replied.

The barkeep pointed out Darren and she followed his direction. Darren watched her walk across the worn carpet to the scarred table where he sat, making overlapping circles of condensation on the table with the bottom of his empty glass. His hat was pulled low, shadowing his eyes. *He thinks he's being sly, watching and no one can see what he's looking at.* As she approached the table, he pushed his hat to the back of his head in a gesture of friendliness. *He looks a little like an old movie star in a cowboy hat. Who was it? Erroll Flynn. That's right. He knows exactly what he's doing to try and charm me.* She slipped into the booth across from him and studied his black, tousled curls. A sure sign that he had been drinking. A lot. He always ran his fingers through his hair when he was drunk. He smiled a lop-sided smile and his eyes crinkled in an attempt at flirtation. She stared at him, unblinking.

"Hello beautiful. It's good to see you."

"What do you want to talk about, Darren?"

He lifted his empty glass in the direction of the bartender.

The proprietor brought two drinks and removed the empty glass before Darren spoke.

"I just want to talk. We have a lot of years together, Carolina. I know that I screwed up. I never meant to hurt you."

"You mean that you never meant to get caught, don't you?"

He ignored her angry words and continued. "No one has ever meant as much to me as you."

She turned from him and stared at the two old men hunched on barstools, watching her reflection in the mirror behind the bar. They lowered their eyes to their drinks. She studied the yellow patterns of light on the smoke-stained walls. *This is the right place for this conversation. Dark, dingy, and depressing.*

Darren slowly stroked his mustache, waiting for her to look at his generous mouth. He licked his lips. "Will you forgive me and let's try again?"

She looked penetratingly into his eyes, ignoring his subterfuge. "Forgiveness has nothing to do with it, Darren. You won't change." Darren reached for her hand where it rested, curled around her glass. She pulled away and put her hand in her lap.

"Darren, this isn't the first time and if I were to stay, it won't be the last."

"Carolina, she meant nothing to me. I love you. I have since the first day I first saw you."

No word of apology. No repentance in his voice. Just a plea that I take him back.

"You have a funny way of showing it. Do you have any idea how I feel knowing that you would throw away our marriage for someone that you say you care nothing for?"

"I wasn't thinking. I promise it won't happen again."

"Words are cheap. I thought you wanted to discuss a settlement."

"The only thing I want to settle is us getting back together."

She studied him sitting there, slouched in the booth, his hair tousled, his crooked grin, his eyes slightly out of focus. *I wonder how much he's had to drink. I don't even miss him. He's just a bad habit.*

The little bit of goodwill that she felt for her husband dissolved quickly before the anger that rose in her at his betrayal and lack of repentance. *He's not going to change; he just doesn't want to lose me.*

It dawned on her that the reason Darren got the upper hand and would convince her to take him back each time was the sound of his voice. It was a deep, seductive. His words rolled over her, covering her like a cloud. He knew how to use it to get his way. It was only now that she had learned to separate his words from his voice that she could stand up to him and hold her ground.

"I want to make it right, Carolina."

"You can do right, but you can't make it right."

"What's the difference?"

Carolina slid from the booth and stood looking down at him. "The fact that you don't know the difference says everything. Goodbye, Darren."

She walked quickly away, ignoring the sound of him calling her name.

"Hi, Liz. This is Carolina. Do you have time to talk?"

"I do, chickadee. How's everything?"

"I just need to talk."

"Of course. What's happening?"

"I feel like I've come to a stopping place. I can't seem to move forward in any direction."

"Not surprising. You're going through a lot right now."

"Right. More and more I feel like I want to go back to my childhood and start over. Find something I've missed or forgotten."

"That's normal. Sometimes I just want to crawl into a hole until it all goes away. I feel like if I could start over, I could make better choices."

"That's it. I just want to start over," Carolina agreed.

"If you started over, you wouldn't know what you know now. You'd probably make the same mistakes. Is this about the baby?"

"No. I still grieve for her but I'm okay. It's about Darren and Travis. I still have feelings for Travis. He kissed me the other night."

"Good going, girl!"

"No. It isn't good. He told me that we could only be friends. But then later we danced and afterwards he kissed me."

"Did you kiss him back?"

"I did. It was just like it used to be."

"Then what?"

"Then nothing. He got in his truck and drove off. It just feels like an unfinished story."

"I think it is. What about Darren?"

"He called and wanted to talk. I met him at the No Name, and he started in with the same old crap. I feel differently about him, Liz. It's like I'm seeing him for the first time."

"How do you feel about him now?"

"He's not going to stop running around. I'm mad. Maybe hurt. I don't know."

"That's called falling out of love, Carolina. Stay mad. It'll get you through this."

"More than that. He wants to fight me for the ranch. Dad said not to worry but I can't help it. I hate the thought of a fight. You know how he is."

"I do. But you're tougher now. How's your dad?"

"That's another thing. His leg is fine but there's something going on with him. I don't know what it is. He won't talk about it. I don't know if he's sick or what."

"He never changes, does he? He'll tell you in time. He always does. Tell you what. Why don't you come up here and I'll take a few days off? We can go dancing or anything else you want. We never did get to run around the last time you were up here. How about a road trip?"

"That sounds good."

"Maybe we can find someone better than what we have or don't have. What do you say about that?"

"I say that's what got me in trouble in the first place. Men are Neanderthals. They aren't interested in romance. They treat us like cars. They only want to take us for a test drive."

"Varoom, varoom."

"Oh Liz. You always make me feel better." Carolina said, laughing. "Thanks for listening. Call me, okay?"

"Will do. Hang tough, Carolina. Love you."

"Love you, too."

Chapter 17
The Cat
1865

Morgan saddled his horse and mounted, waiting for Zeke to take the lead. "It's pretty dry up here. I figured the grass would be better this high up."

"There wasn't much snow in the mountains this year. The panthers come up The River from Mexico and the mountain lions come out of the mountains when it gets dry. Coyotes take their cut. We've lost several calves. The boss wants it taken care of. The back paws of the catamounts are larger than the panther. Just so you know what you're tracking. I spotted a black panther the other day but couldn't get a bead on him. Have you ever hunted cats?"

"Some. They got thick along the San Antonio River in Texas a few years back and were bothering the settlers. We didn't have many in Tennessee."

"Oh? You from Tennessee?"

"Yep. I had a place there. Got burned out. Went to Texas and ended up in the Second Texas Mounted Calvary."

"Were you at Glorieta?"

"I was. Got wounded there. Glad it's all over with. Did you serve?"

"I was out on the plains, keeping the peace. With everyone busy at war, some Indians left the reservation and attacked the settlements."

"Same thing around San Antonio. Does anything happen around here? Dances and such?"

"Yep," Zeke said. "There will be one at the Chatham's in two weeks. You'll probably have to stay with the cows since they're still calving. Those catamounts don't roar like the panthers, so they sneak up close before we find them. That's why we look for the cats. They play hell with the cows at calving time. After this time, we'll take turns watching. For now, the boss is testing you. See if you can follow orders."

"It's been done before."

"Why don't we spread out a ways and cut for sign?"

Morgan turned off to the right and was left with his own thoughts. Thoughts of Sophia. *Was it possible that this ranch that Zeke talked about belonged to Sophia's father? I need to make an excuse to get over there.*

Morgan rode until he felt the air temperature change. Following the breeze from the north, he spotted a small, still lake fed by underground springs. He rode up to water his horse and sat, studying his surroundings. The land to the north rose and fell in large swales, covered in buffalo and sacaton grass. There were other grasses in patches that he had never seen before. Cactus that he could not name. Vicious looking with spines and daggers. Horse cripplers for sure. Tracks of many different animals. Foxes, coyotes, antelope. Studying the tracks of the cattle, he found large cat prints embedded in the mud over the prints of cow hooves. He stepped down and dipped his hand in the lake, wiping his face with the cool water.

Mounting, he made a wide circle around the water, cutting for tracks. He found where the big cat headed toward a stand of trees. He rode slowly, studying the trees, until his horse began to dance nervously, snorting at the strange scent. Walker's ears swiveled back and forth. When the horse swung his head from side to side, Morgan could see his eyes wide with fright.

The nervousness was transmitted to Morgan. The horse bolted. Morgan jerked the horse's head back and the dun began pitching, frantic to get away. Given his head, he ran. Morgan slowly eased the animal to a stop. He stepped off and tied the spooked animal to a tree.

Morgan removed his Spencer from the scabbard, jacked a shell into the chamber and walked back the way he had come. Crossing the trail of the cat, he noted that the mountain lion was dragging something beside it. The hair on the back of his neck stood up. He knew he was being watched. His stomach knotted with fear. He took deep breaths to slow his rapidly beating heart.

Approaching the trees, he looked above his head, searching the tree branches then scanning the ground. He followed the paw prints until they stopped at the base of a white oak. The blink of amber eyes was the only motion to give away the location of the big cat. That and the bloody remains of a newborn calf. The cat lay with his side exposed to Morgan. He turned his head to study the man. In slow motion, Morgan raised the Spencer to his shoulder. The cat hissed a warning. Morgan took a deep breath and let it out to steady his aim.

He squeezed the trigger, and the kick promised a direct hit. The cat jumped up, ran a short, reflexive distance, and fell dead.

Morgan eased up to the animal and waited. He jacked a shell in to the chamber. No movement. He touched the tawny hide with the end of his gun. No response. He walked back to the dun and mounted. At a distance he saw dust rising and knew that Zeke had heard the shot. He waited.

Zeke rode at a lope and reined up next to Morgan. "I heard a shot. Did you get something?"

"Yep." Morgan led Zeke to the kill.

"Damn fine shooting, Donnally. The boss is going to be very happy with you. Maybe we can tan the hide for the bunkhouse floor."

The horses shied as the men struggled to drag the cat toward them. Failing that, the remains were left where they were.

"Maybe one of us can get up here tomorrow and skin him. Probably need to bring the pack mule. The horses won't stand for it. I don't know if we have extra salt and gunpowder to tan this with," Zeke remarked.

"I don't care about it."

As they rode back to the ranch house, the conversation turned to the upcoming dance at the Chatham ranch.

"I used to know a girl named Chatham. The last time I heard from her she was at Fort Marcy. She has dark hair, the color of a rusty wheel but shiny and gun metal eyes. Does that sound like any one at Chatham's?"

Zeke laughed. "That doesn't sound very pretty, Donnally. There is a girl with that color hair and gray eyes, but she's a real stem-winder."

"I didn't want you to get too interested. I've written to her for three years. I intend to pursue her."

"You and the rest of the men in two counties."

Conversation at the cook shack was filled with the adventure of the day.

"How did you find him?" Corky asked.

"How did you sneak up on him, Donnally?" Cookie interjected.

"I cut tracks and followed them. I found the cat under the trees with a fresh kill, and I shot him." Morgan said.

"'Well, I'll be a suck egg dog," Zeke said.

The men pressed him with more questions and hoots of appreciation all around the table. Mr. Randel walked in, and all attention turned to him.

"Nice job, Donnally. Was there only one set of tracks?"

Morgan nodded.

You might as well plan on going with us on Saturday."

Morgan nodded again.

"Did the heavy cows get moved?" Randal asked, turning to Parnell.

"Yes, sir," The foreman said.

Chapter 18

Dance at the Chatham's

1865

At daybreak, a quiet ride around the heavy springers, keeping their distance so as not to spook them, freed the men to head towards the Chatham ranch.

Morgan mounted his horse and waited for the other men to gather. Looking around, Morgan asked Parnell, "Is Mr. Randel coming with us?"

"Yup. He's ahead of us in the wagon. We'll catch up with him on the trail."

Corky and Zeke took the lead, leaving Morgan and Parnell to fall in behind. Soon Corky broke into song.

"In the year twenty-nine when the weather was fine, I first made my way to the sweet fair of Trim. For to sell my fine swine it was my design."

Zeke urged his horse ahead, leaving the songster.

The bits of song drifted towards them.

"She was plump, fat and fair and complete in each limb."

Parnell laughed as he watched Zeke ride ahead. "That damn Corky. He's like a rooster. He starts crowing when the sun comes up and keeps crowing all day."

"He does that," Morgan replied.

A slow lope brought the quartet within sight of the wagon. As Morgan rode alongside, he spotted two large, upholstered chairs and box of apples in the bed of the wagon. Tucked into the corners of the box was a jar of hard candy and a bottle of brandy.

When the Chatham headquarters came into sight, Randel sent the men ahead to announce that they were nearly there.

The riders dismounted and turned their unsaddled horses into the corral. Randel instructed that the chairs be unloaded and set beside the wagon. Zeke removed the candy and liquor from the crate and set them in the seat of a chair.

He picked up the box of apples and carried it to where a group of women were setting a table loaded with assorted dishes.

"Where would you like these apples, Miss Chatham?"

Sophia turned to Zeke with a smile and directed him to set it at the end of the makeshift table. Before he could respond, Parnell stepped between them and removed his hat. He smoothed his hair with one hand. Bowing slightly, he grinned broadly and said, "Hello, Miss Chatham. I am much pleased to see you again. May I say that you look right fetching?"

"You may, Mr. Parnell. A woman never wearies of hearing such things."

Mr. Randel called to the two men and Morgan took the opportunity to step behind her. Speaking softly, he said, "Hello, Sophia."

She froze in place as his voice caressed her name. He watched her turn in slow motion, three years melting away as the woman who had occupied his heart and mind for so long stood looking into his eyes.

"Why, hello, Mr. Donnally," she said, looking around to see who might be watching. She saw her father staring at them. Placing her hand on Morgan's arm, she gently guided him out of earshot of the others.

"Please, may we talk later?" she asked, looking around.

"Of course," Morgan replied with a slight smile.

Morgan walked to the far side of the Rocking-R buckboard and leaned against a cottonwood, his arms folded, watching her from a distance. The older men strolled to the chairs and seated themselves, unaware that Morgan stood in the shadow of the trees.

"I bought a load of cows and three bulls. I'm expecting them next week. They're English stock. I want to breed some of the longhorn out of my cattle. They take too long to grow out and never put on much weight."

"You are an industrious man, Randel. I should follow your lead."

"I figure I can make up the cost of the cattle on the weight gain before long. I have a contract to deliver three hundred head to Fort Sumner in the fall. The cows I've purchased will replace them."

"How about another drink, Chatham?"

"Don't mind if I do."

"There is another matter that I want to discuss with you. I have taken quite a shine to your daughter. I know that I am some older than her, but I would like your permission to court her."

The silence that filled the air swirled around Morgan. *Zeke warned me that there were many men trying to court her. I never imagined that one of them would be my boss.*

Morgan wanted to listen to the rest of the conversation, but good manners required that he make himself known.

He stepped around the tail gate and greeted the men. Without indicating that he had heard anything, he continued walking toward the banquet table.

The men looked at each other as Morgan stepped past them to the makeshift kitchen.

The dinner bell rang, and everyone gathered around the tables. Mr. Randel said a blessing over the food and prayed for rain. Sophia's dad approached her, gestured in the direction of Mr. Randel and said that she should take two plates and join the man. She turned, searching, and her eyes met Morgan's. She gave a slight shrug and went to the seat vacated by her father.

Mr. Chatham saw the gesture and turned to face Morgan. Morgan met his gaze then turned to join the other men, squatting in the group. He bent his head to his plate and played with his food, ignoring the icy stare of the older man.

Avoiding Sophia, who was being closely watched by her father, he offered his assistance in moving the tables to the side of the house, clearing an area for the night's festivities. The women were busy, covering the food, putting the young children down to sleep, and mixing a large bowl of punch for the party. The small band of musicians tuned up and practiced quietly.

Morgan stood in the shadows of the house and watched Mr. Randel offer his hand to Sophia. They began to dance. At the end of their dance, another cowboy stepped forward and she danced with one then another until she pleaded exhaustion. She helped herself to a cup of punch and stood watching the other dancers, smiling, looking around. Morgan approached her and with a slight bow, asked for a waltz.

He had never held her. She was warm and supple. He inhaled the lavender scent of her. The intoxication of having her so close after all this time choked him with emotion. Too soon the dance was over, and she was swept away into a schottische.

All of the men, eager to dance, kept the women and older girls dancing in the dirt. Dust from the hard-packed ground soon formed a cloud, causing everyone to cough and run for the punch bowls. Two men with buckets sprinkled water across the dance area, settling the dust. Morgan took the opportunity to reach for Sophia's elbow and direct her away from the crowd.

"I want to talk to you. Will you take some time for me?"

"My father has instructed me to take care of our guests. I will encourage him and Mr. Randel to return to their bottle. Then we can walk."

Mr. Randel appeared and regained his seat beside Mr. Chatham. "How about another drink, Chatham?"

"Pleased to do it, Randel."

"I can't keep up with her in the dance department, but I assure you, I will take care of her and she will never know want."

"I know you will. She's headstrong, so go easy with her. She was raised without a mother. That's why I sent her off to school. You'll have to win her over."

Morgan retreated to the trees and continued to watch her. Sophia approached the seated men. Morgan watched as she smiled and poured a drink for her father and suitor. She soon slipped into the shadows with Morgan. He reached for her hand and stood in the darkness, looking into eyes that matched the moonlit sky.

"Sophia, I have waited three years to do this."

He bent his head to her and gently touched her lips, pulling her against him with rising urgency. She put her hand on his chest and pushed away.

"Not here. Not now."

"When can I see you?"

"Father has encouraged me to accept Mr. Randel. I've resisted but..."

"I want to marry you. I want to take care of you. I have nothing right now, but please wait. I'll figure something. I don't know what, but I can't lose you. Not after all this time. Please, Sophia."

She touched his face and he reached to hold her hands.

"We go to town every third Tuesday of the month. Father meets his friends for business, cards, and drinking. Sometimes we spend the night. I usually shop. I can meet you in town then."

"I'll be there."

Morgan held both of her hands to his chest then kissed each finger.

Her eyes were glistening when she turned to go.

Mr. Randel called for the men to gather up. They loaded the chairs and retrieved their horses. The hands sat quietly on their saddled mounts, watching the boss attempt to crawl unsteadily aboard the wagon.

Parnell said, "Corky, you drive and let Mr. Randel rest." Corky tied his horse to the tailgate and climbed up beside his inebriated boss. The men gave the horses their heads and they were soon lined out, headed for home. Even Corky had run out of songs.

"Parnell, I need to go to town next Tuesday, if you don't mind."

"Is this something that can wait until payday, Donnally?"

"No, I can stay and work next payday, but I really need to get to town on Tuesday."

"Well, I guess you can ride in with the boss."

"I'd rather not. I'll ride in early and be back before he is."

Parnell studied Morgan. "I guess that will be alright. Is anything wrong?"

"No. Just something I need to take care of."

Morgan woke before daylight and lay listening to the steady breathing of the men. Corky's snore elicited a kick to his bunk from Zeke. When the quiet had been restored, Morgan felt for the money he had stashed in his mattress and removed it. Cautiously, he slid from his bunk and pulled on his boots. Finding his coat, he slipped out of the bunkhouse and headed for the tack room.

He roped and saddled his horse, easing him out of the corral to the nicker of the other horses. He mounted and walked the horse out of hearing of the ranch house before urging the animal into a slow trot.

The roll of the horse in the cool morning air cleared Morgan's mind and he searched for a plan that would give him enough money to fulfill his promise to Sophia. It wouldn't be easy. *Maybe the burned-out place in Tennessee might be worth something if the carpetbaggers haven't taken it. I don't have enough money to go back and see about that yet. I wonder if Mr. Randel would let me buy a couple of horses to keep on the ranch to use for trade?* Ideas tumbled desperately through his mind as he rode through the emerging light of morning.

The town was beginning to stir when Morgan entered the small settlement. Riding up to the livery, he dismounted and called for service. An old cowpuncher emerged from the barn, pitchfork in hand. The rolling gait and worn attire spoke of years in the saddle. His scuffed boots left clouds of dust as he failed to lift his feet. He was a thin, inelegant man who carried himself erect like someone who had lost everything but his dignity.

"Mornin'. What can I do for you?"

"I just need to feed and leave him here for a while."

"Out back." The man gestured to the corral. "I'll take care of him directly."

Morgan strolled along the boardwalk and peered in windows, waiting for the Mercantile to open. When the clerk unlocked the store, he followed him in, not wanting to spend unnecessary time on the street, where he might be seen. He looked among the clothing and selected some socks and a blue striped shirt.

He had not had any new clothes since before the war. He looked in the mirror behind the counter and was distraught at his appearance. His worn military drab hat sat shapeless on his head. His threadbare, gray shirt hung limp under his scarred leather vest.

"Would you mind if I changed my shirt right here? I didn't realize how worn mine is."

The clerk looked around the store and out the window. "Well, that is out of the ordinary, but I guess you can step into the back and change."

The clerk, watching Morgan study himself in the mirror, suggested a new hat to go with the new shirt.

"Can't do that just yet. Need to wait until payday."

After completing his purchases and changing into the new shirt, he stood with his string tied bundle tucked under his arm, looking out of the window. He beat the dust from his military issue drab Kepi and fingered it into a recognizable form. He licked his finger and smoothed the frayed soutache braid. There wasn't anything he could do about the cracked leather. He made a mental note to try some saddle soap on it when he got back to the ranch. The clerk watched Morgan where he stood searching the street.

"Is there anything else I can do for you, sir?"

"No. I'm just waiting for someone."

"Perhaps you could see them better from the bench outside," the man said, his voice breaking.

Morgan turned and looked at the clerk, weighing the meaning and tone of his words. "Have a good day," he said as he stepped outside and walked to the livery. He put his purchases in his saddle bags and leaned on the saddle. Using the leather thong, which was tied to a buttonhole, he pulled his father's pocket watch from his vest and watched the road he had recently traveled.

It was late morning before he spotted the wagon with Sophia and her father. Morgan stepped into the barn to avoid being seen by his employer. He watched as Sophia was handed down from the wagon by Mr. Randel. She disappeared inside the hotel. Mr. Chatham drove the rig to the livery to be left in the care of the liveryman.

Sophia emerged from the hotel and searched the store fronts. Her father and Mr. Randel were deep in conversation with two other men. Their voices, as they entered the hotel lobby, drifted across the nearly vacant street with talk of railroads and cattle. Her step lightened as she walked out of sight of the hotel. She strolled along the boardwalk. Looking in a store window, she studied her reflection and lifted a hand to smooth an errant wisp of hair. The window glass reflected the scene behind her, and she studied it, searching. Sophia entered the general store to leave a list for the clerk to fill, then paused at the door, scanning the street. Walking along the boardwalk she entered the Mercantile. She left a list of ranch supplies to be filled and turned to leave.

Morgan stepped up and opened the door for her, touching the brim of his hat. "Where can we go?" he whispered, the blood rushing in his ears.

"The Capitol, down the street," she replied, brushing past him.

They walked side by side, without speaking, until they reached their destination. Morgan opened the door to the quiet cafe, stood close and inhaled the scent of her as she passed by.

A waitress eyed the couple when they sat down in a corner, away from the window. Morgan tucked his cap behind him in his belt.

"What can I get for you folks?"

"Two coffees, please." Morgan said.

They sat there, at a corner of the table, the years of waiting enveloped them in a cloud of desire as they gazed into each other's eyes.

Morgan cleared his throat, searching for words. The silence was full. She waited expectantly, staring up into his anxious face. Sorting out his words, he finally spoke. "Sophia, you have been in my heart and mind for over three years. I hope my letters made clear to you my intentions. Seeing you with anyone else is more than I can bear. Wait a little longer. I'll figure out something."

"Morgan, please don't let it be long. My father is anxious that I accept Mr. Randel's proposal. If I marry him, I'll stay close to my father. I'm all that he has. That way, the ranches will be joined."

"Sophia, say you'll wait until I can get things gathered up. That cursed war has turned everything upside down. I lost everything."

"I know, my love."

Her words surprised and delighted him. Clasping her hands, he held them tight. He turned them over, kissed the inside of her wrists then looked around, embarrassed by his emotional display.

Time slipped by as they spoke quietly to each other, both keenly aware of each moment passing.

"Will you have more coffee, or would you care to eat?" asked the waitress, looking pointedly around at the tables that were now rapidly being filled.

"I believe we have had an elegant sufficiency," replied Morgan. Sophia lifted her pendant watch from between her breasts. "It's almost twelve o'clock, Morgan. I should go. Father will be expecting me for dinner."

Morgan cupped her hand in his, pretending to study the watch. The pink guillione face was dotted with seed pearls and tourmaline. He gently rubbed his fingers over it as he caressed her hand.

"It belonged to my mother."

"Beautiful," he said, looking into her eyes. "Remember your promise."

"I will. You do the same."

The shadows were long when Morgan returned to headquarters. Parnell studied him as he unsaddled and turned his horse into the corral.

Entering the cook shack together, Parnell greeted the men and waited until everyone served themselves. He asked for an account of the day's activities.

Corky and Zeke described the tracks they had seen, and the calf remains they had found.

"Morgan, do you have anything to report?"

"No. All is well."

"You should know that Mr. Randel wants you to go with him to Denver next month. There will be a general auction of surplus military gear and horses. He wants you to look them over."

"How are we getting up there?"

"By train. Mr. Chatham and his daughter are also going. You'll ride back with the horses, by train. Mr. Randel will wire us when to expect you and we'll meet you at the pens in town to drive them back here."

"Will do."

"Day after tomorrow we start gathering on the Conogar place. We need to be set up at the bottom of the bluffs by tomorrow afternoon. The Conogar and Donlevy crews will there."

"It'll be good to see some new faces," Zeke said, looking around.

"Well, you don't have to look at yours until you shave, which ain't too often." Corky retorted.

"I'll see you ladies in the morning." Parnell rose and left the table.

Chapter 19
Gathering in the Ravine
1865

The Rocking R wagon rolled up to the selected campground and Cookie eased himself down. "Here comes the old woman and Little Mary," said Zeke, referring to the cook and his helper.

"Better not let Cookie hear you say that," Parnell warned.

The men and Cookie's helper gathered what mesquite wood and cow chips they could find. Corky could be heard singing. "Did you ever, ever, ever, in your long-legged life, see a long-legged sailor with his long-legged wife?"

"Do you think if a horse kicked him on the other side of the head, he would stop that squalling?" Zeke quipped.

"The Conogar crew will know that we're here soon enough," Parnell said, chuckling.

"It's a good thing we're not trying to surprise anyone," Morgan replied.

Darkness settled around the campfires and the men from three camps gathered to exchange news and stories. Someone got out a guitar and singing could be heard as the glow of cigarettes dotted the camp sites. A deck of cards appeared and some of the men gathered around a blanket. Money appeared and the evening was spent losing and winning.

"Everyone better turn in, we start at first light," Parnell announced.

The heavy morning air held the smells of breakfast close to the ground. The men rose from their bedrolls and tied them up, tossing them in the wagons as they passed by for a plate of beef and potatoes.

Breakfast complete, they chose their mounts and saddled. Some of the horses bucked and crow hopped, froggy in the early morning chill. The men sat their horses and were waiting for instructions by the time the sun crept over the horizon. The three foremen sat their horses, facing the men. Parnell called for everyone's attention.

"Listen up, boys. Two men from Donlevy's outfit will hold the bottom of the box canyon. Don't let them through. The rest of Donlevy's men will start in the hills and push the cattle down toward the canyon. Chatham's group will start in the east from The River and do the same. The Rafter R will go north to the lake and push south to the canyon. Any questions?"

Silence greeted him. "All right then. Let's ride."

The day passed quickly with hazing and brush popping as the men found and drove the cattle toward the deep ravine. The countenance of the rock faces was stern, watchful, echoing the sounds of bawling and the clack of horns as the cattle jockeyed for space. The herd leaders shied from the shadows that pushed the daylight back against the sky.

The cowboys fanned out and pressed forward. Parnell pulled his hat from his head and gestured with it to the outriders signaling them to slow down. He called out to those who were near. "Slow them down, we don't want them spilling out the other end."

Deer bounded out of the ravine. The cattle began to slow, not feeling the pressure to move forward. A thin stream wandered through the canyon. The cottonwoods cast shadows across the slough. The sun was slipping down the western sky when the three groups converged at the head of the canyon.

"Good job men. We need two on each end to hold them. Two hour watches all night. Everyone else go eat."

Parnell and Morgan took the first watch on the north end.

"You'll learn new habits here, Morgan. It's an unforgiving land. That's why some Easterners don't make it."

"I can see that. Some land doesn't forgive incompetence or ignorance."

"You're right about that. Here's a couple of things you might not have seen in Tennessee. Follow the trail of coyotes and other critters, they will show you where there's water. Also, the bottle cactus, if you can find them, hold water."

"Thanks for the advice. It might come in handy."

"What's that long gun you carry?"

"It's a Spencer repeater."

"I've seen some of the Henrys that the South issued but never saw a Spencer."

Morgan pulled the gun from his scabbard and handed it to Parnell.

"Where did you get it?" asked Parnell, examining the steel frame rifle. "I see it's not brass."

"No, it's Union made. I took it off a dead Yank. Shells are a little hard to find. I bought a box of loose shells, but they make a tube with seven shells. It makes loading faster."

"Does it shoot better?"

"I think so. It's a seven-shot repeater. The Henry carries sixteen but the wood under the barrel on this one makes it easier to hold. It doesn't get hot. That was a real problem during the war."

"Damn!" Parnell said in a tone of admiration, handing it back to him.

Corky and Zeke rode across the ridge to spell Parnell and Morgan, leaving them free to return to camp. They could hear the sound of a guitar being played as they rode down the rocky bluff. They unsaddled and received a plate of beef and beans from Cookie, topped with two biscuits. Parnell spied the remains of a peach cobbler and said, "Cookie, don't let that get away before we have a pass at it."

Morgan laid down and leaned against his saddle. The howling of the coyotes and the conversing of the night denizens filled the darkness. He watched the grass shimmering silver in the moonlight and listened as the silence settled on the campsite until the sound of men snoring lulled him to sleep.

The smells of breakfast on the fire lured the men from their bedrolls, accompanied by groans and muttered swearing.

A commotion in the Donlevy camp brought everyone to attention.

"What the hell's happenin' over there?"

"One ole boy is getting chapped."

"Looks like he rode his horse inside the camp circle."

"That'll do it. Don't he know to stay a lariat length away from the cook wagon?"

"I bet he does now."

The men whooped and hollered as the offender was whipped with his own chaps. Parnell interrupted the merriment and gave instructions. Two men to relieve the night riders on each end.

"Morgan, do you rope worth a damn?"

"I do other things a lot better. Why don't I spell the night riders at the top? This is a trail horse. He doesn't know cutting." He did not mention that a previous broken leg might hinder his working on the ground with the branding iron.

Parnell nodded and watched as Morgan and Corky rode toward the bluffs. He then split the crew, assigning the jobs of cutting out the calves, roping and dragging them to the fire. Two men were assigned to keep any angry mamas from running over the working men.

The work proceeded quickly as the men fell into the rhythm of the tasks at hand. They began cutting out the mamas and calves to separate them from the herd. Small bunches of cows and calves that did not belong on Chatham's range were driven at a distance from the herd and held. Roping the calves and dragging them to the fire soon began. The crews fell into a routine and their timing left little room for mistakes or missed throws.

Mr. Chatham sat horseback beside Parnell as he counted the cows with their calves. They were run by him at the end of the day.

"Three fifty-seven, sir. Probably that many more to be worked tomorrow."

"They look good, Parnell."

"Lots of grass still in the valleys and in the hills. That's why it took so long to get them gathered. Are you staying with us tonight, sir?"

"No. I'm going back to the house. I'm too old to sleep on the ground. See you tomorrow evening."

"Yes, sir."

The worn-out cowboys kicked dirt on the branding fires and drew matchsticks to choose who would take the first watch, leaving the rest to gather around the cooks' fires for supper.

Corky said, "I sure could use some scrumpy ale. It makes my legs go funny."

"Shut up, Corky!" Zeke commanded, annoyance and exhaustion evident in his voice.

"Yes sir, I sure could use some scrumpy ale," Corky whispered to himself, rubbing his back.

A subdued crew soon found their bedrolls and rolled into them for the night. The men worked from can see to can't see. The night hawks could be heard singing softly as they rode slowly around the herd.

The men trailed into the cook shack still weary from the three days of intense work.

"I'm so hungry my belly thinks my throat's been cut," Zeke said.

"I had to punch another hole in my belt," added Corky.

Parnell entered and greeted the cowboys gathered around the table. "Good job, men. We held our own. We'll work Donlevy's cattle next week. Mr. Randel wants to wait until he gets back from his trip to work ours. Three hundred steers, yearling or better, and old cows will be cut for a road trip. Use your best judgement."

Chapter 20
Fire on Travis's Ranch
2012

"Morgan here," he said groggily into the phone.

"Morgan, I need your help," Travis said. "There's a fire in the east pasture. I'm taking the tractor to cut a line. If I can make a fire break, I might get it stopped. I called Tom. He's bringing a fire tanker. He said he'd call Eldrige to bring the other one. They'll call the other volunteers. It'll take a while for them to get out here."

Morgan listened to the anxious instructions, waiting until Travis ran out of words before speaking.

"What do you want me to do?"

"If you can move the cattle into the home pasture for me, it would help a lot. I'm leaving the gate open. Push them in there."

"I'll get it done, Travis. Carolina will help. You take care of your end, my friend."

Morgan dressed and tapped on Carolina's open bedroom door.

Carolina awoke with a start, "What is it, Dad?"

"Travis has a grass fire. He needs us to move the cattle into the house pasture. Are you in?"

"Of course. I'll pack. Meet you at the truck."

She knew from years of riding with him what he would have in the truck and what she would need. *More water, of course. Everything else would be in the pickup. Wild rags, first aid, flashlights, tools.* Her mind raced through emergencies they had in the past. Morgan's words echoed in her head. *'I would rather have it and not need it than need it and not have it.' What would they need? More water, yes. Maybe some biscuits. What else?* Her heart was in her throat as she scrambled to gather everything she could. Long-sleeved shirt, light jacket, gloves, spurs. She tied her hair up under a ball cap to get it out of the way.

By the time she met him at the truck, he had saddled and loaded one of the horses. The black, Hunter, stood quietly in the trailer. The roan colt shied and fought his head. Morgan backed him down, talking to him, a hand on his neck to calm the young horse. He walked the roan into the trailer and stepped out the side door. Carolina closed the trailer gate. *I wish we had Walker, but the old horse won't hold up to the ride.* The older, experienced horses were unlikely to panic under good riders. There was a lariat tied to each saddle and a scabbard on Morgan's. She noticed that he had put a rifle in the truck. It chilled her. *He must be expecting the worst if he has to carry that. Oh God, please don't let him need it.*

They sped to the burning pasture and unloaded Hunter. He was nervous but steady and turned to face the fire. Morgan tied him to the trailer. The roan, agitated, stomping with his front feet in the trailer, would not unload. Morgan stepped in the side door and began to ease the horse backwards. He slowly backed the young horse, talking to him, stroking his neck until he stepped on to the ground. Carolina watched her dad handle the fractious animal. His words from the past came to mind. *'The fastest way to work animals is slow.'* Morgan struggled to hold on to him as he spoke to Carolina with his mouth close to her ear so she could hear him over the wind and fire. "Carolina, wet that rag and cover your face." He watched as she pulled the jug from the truck and poured water onto the bandanna wadded in her hand.

"Not like that. Put it over your nose. Tie it tight. Pull your cap down. Put your gloves on." He handed Carolina the reins to the nervous roan and wet his kerchief.

She studied him as he reached under the truck seat and felt for his spurs. He fastened them on his boots and straightened up. When he turned around his hat was pulled down tight on his head. He appeared comical with the flowered print of the bandanna covering his face. She looked into his intense, worried eyes and knew he was not smiling.

"Are you all right?"

Carolina nodded. Fear held her tongue in the back of her throat. She bent to put on her spurs and hide her face from her father.

"Watch which way the fire is moving. We'll start as close as we can to the fire and push the cattle toward the house. The gate will be open, so don't worry about slowing them down. They won't hurt themselves if we don't crowd them. The old cows know where the gate is. They'll lead the point. Use your rope. Don't waste time on any of them that want to fight. Above all, look out for yourself. Are you okay?"

Worry in his voice transferred to her and she fought against the panic.

She nodded, again.

He squeezed her shoulder. "Let's go. Everything will be fine."

She was not so sure.

Carolina swung into her saddle and watched her dad mount the skittish horse. As the adrenaline flowed into her, she pulled her lariat free of the leather thong and shook the loop into a knot with a flick of her wrist. The light of the moon was blurred by the dust and the smoke, barely revealing the outline of the cows as they rose and began bawling for their calves. Nervous and watchful, they bunched up, facing her, perceiving her to be the most immediate danger.

She rode toward them, whooping and swinging her rope, turning them westward. The bawling of cows and calves added to the cacophony of other sounds filling the hot night air.

The leaders began to sort themselves out. The herd turned and moved in unison. She continued loping north along the fire line. She could see the pinpoint of lights from Travis's tractor moving slowly in the far distance. Her heart went out to him. *How must he feel to be fighting to save his grass, his livelihood, his family? I wonder where the girls are. They must be with their grandmother.*

Carolina turned her attention to the cattle. *This is the most good I can do for him right now.* She loosened the reins and nudged Hunter into a canter, swinging the rope end at every cow and calf she found. The fire created its own wind, pushing it westward towards Travis's home and family.

Carolina's nose burned from the odorous stench of the creosote bushes igniting and throwing flames upward, sending sparks to the smoke-filled, starless sky. The creosote flared like the Biblical burning bush. She thought she heard a shot and turned to see an explosion of fireworks, spraying an arc of colors from the top of a power pole.

She pulled up for a moment to look around. The specks of light that showed her where the house pasture was had disappeared. *There won't be any power at the house. I hope the old cows know where the gate is. I can't tell.*

The sound of the cattle drowned out her own voice. Wisps of hair escaped her cap and stuck to her sweaty face. Her eyes stung and watered from the acrid smoke. The wild rag filtered the ashes but not the caustic air. Her throat began to burn, and the colorful bandanna was dry. It was getting harder to breathe. She spit into the cloth that clung to her mouth, trying to wet it.

Carolina reached the north fence and wheeled the horse around, patting him as she let him stand and blow. *Dad would tell me to slow him down, don't use him up.* She stroked his lathered neck until his labored breathing slowed, then urged him on at a trot, easier on him but harder on her, riding the undulating rolls of land. She rode through the dust and smoke, checking the lower ground and ravines. Topping the knolls, she stood in the saddle, searching in the darkness.

She cut across the pasture at an angle, following the cattle as they headed westward. The night seemed to go on forever at a reckless pace.

Rabbits, field mice, sage hens and quail, coyotes and every other creature of the prairie ran in panic before the encroaching fire. The hunted and the hunter, terrified. A snake slithered under her horse. He jumped. She held on to the saddle.

The bawling, the coughing, the rumble of the gathering hooves filled her ears. Adrenaline surged through her, clearing her head. Her only thought was to keep the cattle from turning back.

After hours of riding, a dirty light was lifting in the east. The outline of two fire tankers and several pickups were visible at the edge of the smoldering grass. She could barely make out the figures of one man on the front of each truck, holding a fire hose, chasing the flames. Silhouettes of men could be seen working furiously along the line, putting out the many fires which caught and flamed as they found nourishment in the dry tufts of grass. The orange line was no longer sweeping westward, hindered now by the disced-up ground that Travis had sacrificed to halt the menace.

The last of the cattle went through the gate. Carolina waited there, praying. She positioned herself so that her horse funneled the next wave of cows, driven by Morgan, through the gate. She sat, her hands on the pommel, until she saw her dad emerge through the smoky haze, yelling, swinging his rope, driving the cattle before him. She could barely hear him over the bawling of the cows, frantic to keep track of their calves. She followed the last of them through the gate. Morgan reined his horse and made a thumbs up gesture. He swung down, pulled the gate around and tied it shut behind him. He walked weak-kneed toward her and laid his hand on her leg.

"Are you all right, Carolina?"

She nodded, her lips quivering, her eyes watering. The adrenaline had drained from her body, leaving her weak and shaking. She dared not dismount for fear of falling.

He reached up, slipped his hands around her waist and caught her as she slid from the saddle, easing her to the ground.

The horses stood, heads down, their lathered sides heaving, coughing with hoarse rasping sounds, their knees quivering. She knew how they felt.

"You did a fine job, Carolina. You'll do to ride the river with."

She knew there was no higher praise than that. She fought back tears of relief. They stood still. He held her, with her face buried against him until she could stand by herself. Reaching around her neck, he gently untied the bandanna and began to wipe her face.

"I must be an unholy mess, Dad," she said, coughing.

"You look beautiful." He choked.

She studied her father's face. The soot had left an ashen cloak over his entire body that blended with the sky. The upper part of his face was dark and dirty. The lower half, which had been covered, was streaked with sweat and grime. His gray eyes were blood shot and red-rimmed. Gray and brown stubble gave him a rugged, untamed look. The blue flowered wild rag, filthy now, hung loosely around his neck. She began to laugh uncontrollably.

Morgan hugged her, squeezed her hard then held her by the shoulders at arm's length. "Carolina, I need to go get the trailer and see if I can help. All right?" She nodded, afraid to speak. Morgan lifted her chin and kissed her on the forehead.

"You'll be fine. Unsaddle Hunter and put him in the corral for now. It shouldn't take long. I need to see how the fire line is doing."

Carolina led Hunter to the corral, not trusting herself to mount the tall horse again. She unsaddled, turned him in, and watched as he rolled in the dirt. *I should at least brush him. He deserves to be hosed down, but I can't do that because the electricity is out. No water.* She sat on the fence rail and promised him that he would be well-groomed when they got home. Watching the tractor lights moving along the orange line gave her time to think about Travis and that kiss at the Armory. *What did he mean by that? Anything?*

She watched the lights of the tractor and a line of headlights moving across the pasture, followed by the fire trucks. The procession of vehicles was hidden in a cloud of dust rising from the dry ground. She hurried to open the gate. As they drove in, each driver lifted a weary hand in salute.

Morgan stepped out of his pickup and stood beside her. "Okay?"

"Yes, Dad. How's Travis?"

"He'll make it."

When the last fire truck drove through the gate, Morgan pulled it shut and unloaded the roan, tied him to the trailer and removed his saddle. They walked slowly, side by side, toward the men gathering in the front yard.

Morgan spoke up. "Travis, I don't think we missed very many. I shot one that had her horns caught in the fork of a tree. At least it isn't early spring. The calves were big enough to follow the mamas. I know that we got the bulls."

His eyes locked with Morgan's in unspoken gratitude. "Thanks," was all Travis could say, coughing to mask the break in his voice.

He grasped Morgan's hand in a tight grip and grabbed his forearm. Morgan did the same. The universal sign of brotherhood.

The men were beginning to gather, talking among themselves about the night. Travis looked around, searching for Carolina.

"I better get started making some sandwiches. Carolina, do you want to help me make some coffee?"

She nodded and followed him to the house. He reached for her hand, guiding her in the dark kitchen. When they were out of sight of the men, Travis pulled her to him, burying his face in her neck. She could feel his tears.

She touched his chin, guiding his face to her mouth.

"Cee," he whispered hoarsely. She froze. He hadn't called her that in years.

"Thank God it's over, Travis."

"This part is," he replied.

She wrapped her arms around him and could feel him tremble.

Pulling away from her, he fumbled in a drawer saying, "I better find some candles."

He placed them on the table and felt around for the holders. Finding them, he stood them firmly in the glass receptacles and lit three tapers. In the flickering illumination, they gathered sandwich making supplies.

"I'll start the coffee, so when the lights come back on it'll be ready," said Carolina.

"Good idea."

She looked up at him. His amber eyes were bloodshot and wet. He wiped them with the back of his blackened hands, smearing the ash and dirt to his temples. She clung to his soot-filled shirt, not wanting to embarrass him. They stood like that, not speaking until he quit shaking. They pulled apart and she studied his face. The raccoon markings on his tanned face created a comic picture. She shuddered and began to laugh. He joined her nervously.

"Are the girls asleep?" Carolina asked.

"Probably. The first thing I did was take them to Mom's house. I'm sure she'll be over here as soon as the lights come back on."

He had only just said it when the lights flickered and glowed, revealing the absurd sight of the soot-covered pair and the magnitude of what they had gone through.

Travis took a kitchen towel from the handle of the stove and wet it. He tenderly washed her face until he had wiped away the track of her tears. She took it from him and wet the other end. She gently wiped his face, the towel catching in the copper stubble on his chin. Travis kissed her, and they clung together with no sound except the coffee hissing its way through the machine.

The sound of Katherine's voice made them jump apart.

"Are you two going to get those sandwiches built or stand there necking?"

"Hi, Mom. I guess we're doing both. Are the girls asleep?"

"Yes. I left a note for them in case they wake up. Let's get busy with those sandwiches, kids. Do you have any Joy Juice, Travis? Some of the men might appreciate a shot of flavoring in their coffee."

Travis nodded and retrieved the bottle from a high shelf.

A sheriff's car pulled up and Greg Carrasco stepped out. "Well! Our local gendarme," someone said under his breath. The deputy pushed out his chest and strode to the group, walking in a practiced manner, meant to impress, intimidate. He looked down, being careful where he stepped.

"Well, it looks like it could have been a lot worse," he said smugly.

Morgan blocked Carrasco's passage to the house.

"How can I help you, Greg?"

"I am here in my official capacity," he said, testily. "I want to talk to Travis."

"He's busy right now. Why don't you interview the others and by the time you're finished Travis should be out here?"

"Are you trying to tell me how to do my job, Donnally?"

"No, I'm just suggesting that you start with the other witnesses while Travis takes care of some things." Morgan hooked his thumbs in his front pockets and stood flat-footed on the porch, staring down at the younger man.

Carrasco turned to the group of men who encircled him. "Does anyone know how it started?"

Tom stepped forward to answer questions while Carrasco took field notes. "Either a cigarette or someone pulled off the road into the grass. Those catalytic converters sometimes start fires. At least someone spotted it and called Travis."

The other men came forward and volunteered information until the officer turned around, his face still tight with anger. "Now for the tender Travis."

Travis appeared in the doorway. "Here I am, tender or not. But well done." He slowly stepped down to ground level and stood in front of the officer.

"I have questions for you. Let's step aside." Travis followed him away from the others and Morgan glanced around to find Carolina looking after the two men.

"I can't stand that man. Even when we were in school."

"He doesn't stand very tall," Morgan replied.

She knew he was talking about his measure as a man and not his height.

The men stood silent until the officer got into his car. As Carrasco's car pulled away someone said, "There goes a ten-cent man." The men nodded silently.

Katherine appeared with a tray of sandwiches balanced in one hand and a coffee pot in the other.

"Who wants coffee? We have some flavoring of the bourbon variety for anyone who wants it."

Carolina followed behind with a tray of cups and the bottle of spirits. She raised the tray as proof of the offer. The men gathered around and helped themselves to the sandwiches and coffee.

Katherine said, "I'm going to take some sandwiches to the spotters on the line." She headed back to the house to gather more food and thermoses of coffee.

Morgan stood beside Carolina. Travis reached for her hand. They watched as everyone grabbed a sandwich, grateful that the talk had turned away from what they had just been through.

Carrying food and coffee, the men ambled out until they formed a loose line, facing the burned pasture. The wind scattered the smoke-filled clouds and the sun emerged, exposing the night of woe. The men stood silent, side by side, companions, friends, warriors of the range.

Morgan got two buckets, put a shot of shampoo in with the sponges and filled them with water. Carolina crawled through the rails and picked up a sponge. Hunter fidgeted. She laid a steady hand on his neck. Talking to him, she started with a soapy sponge under his mane and worked her way around the horse, ending with his head.

"I guess Hunter isn't used to getting a bath."

"I don't remember the last time. This colt has probably never had one. As the old saying goes, wild and woolly and full of fleas and never been curried below the knees."

"I never heard that before. That's funny... Dad, when are you going to give that horse a name?"

"The only names I've come up with are not very nice. I'm waiting for him to do something good."

"He did a good job last night, didn't he?"

"Yes, he did. For a green horse he did pretty good."

"Well, we don't want to call him green. How about smoke?"

"Except that he's a roan."

"Maybe not fire, but how about fire jumper?"

"Jumper would work. Or Buck. He does a lot of that."

"Buck it is, then. Have you talked to Travis today?"

"Yes. He's riding his pasture."

"Should we help?"

"I asked him. He wants to do it alone."

"Do what?"

"He needs to assess the damage and figure out what to do about it. He may also have to put down any wounded animals."

"I didn't think of that. Can't we help?"

"No. It's like grief. He's mourning. He needs to get a handle on what happened and what could have happened. He'll be all right in a few days. Just give him space."

"My heart hurts for him. I wish I knew what to do."

"It'll come to you. I'm finished with Buck. When you get finished why don't we go to town and catch a movie and supper."

"I would love that, Dad."

Two weeks later Morgan and Carolina pulled up and parked beside the barn on Travis's ranch. They carried bowls of potato salad and banana pudding through the open doors.

"Well! Good to see you two. What do you have here?" Katherine asked, peeking into the bowls.

"Where did you get all of these tables and chairs, Katherine?" Carolina asked.

"From the Bingo Hall. We don't need to have them back until Wednesday. It certainly is a blessing."

"I love the decorations. You put a lot of work into this," Caroline said, looking around.

"It was little enough to do."

"Katherine, what can we do to help?" Morgan asked.

"If Carolina will help me finish bringing out the food from the house, that would be great. And Morgan- Travis is checking on the beef in the pit. It's about done. He may need some help with that. If you could set up some hay bales for more seating, that would be good."

Mona and Eldrige appeared with two kids tagging behind. "Here's a bowl of whistle berries," Eldrige said, placing the bowl of beans on the table.

"Smells good, Mona," Katherine said, smiling.

As the rest of the firefighters and their families began showing up with food, the barn filled with talk and laughter. Soon platters of beef were set on the serving table. Travis hollered above the noise for attention. Everyone began to gather into a circle around Travis and his mother. Carly and Callie stood in front of their dad, his hands resting on their heads.

"Friends, I am at a loss for words to express how Mom and I feel about what y'all have done. Without all your help I can't imagine what would've happened. With the wind blowing like it was, I was in trouble, for sure." Travis turned away.

"Ain't no big thing, just chicken wings," Eldrige volunteered. Mona poked him in the ribs.

Katherine spoke up. "That's what makes this the greatest place in the world to live. Having good friends like all of you. Y'all have been such a blessing to our family. A great big thank you from our hearts will have to do until you're better paid. How about a word of thanksgiving?" She turned to Travis.

"Mom, I can't," Travis whispered.

"Morgan, would you do the honors?" Katherine asked.

Morgan nodded and stepped up beside Travis. Placing his hands on the shoulders of Katherine and Travis he began. "Father, we give thanks this day for these friends and this food. We come humbly before you to give thanks for bringing Travis and his family through this ordeal. Please continue to guide them as they work through the trials ahead. Give them strength and discernment. Father, we sure do need some rain. Please keep your hand on those who work in your service and those who suffer for your name. In the name of your Son. Amen."

Katherine reached up, patted his hand and said, "Let's eat, everyone."

A round of applause and heartfelt good wishes were called out from the crowd. Words downplaying their efforts were expressed.

"Glad we could help, Travis. You would have done the same."

"I would, Carl."

That was the way of the men. Minimizing their own part in the matter, glad for the camaraderie.

The crowd began to line up with plates in hand.

"Travis, is this one of the beeves that was barbequed that night?" The group fell silent.

"Eldrige! Don't you have a lick of sense?" Mona hissed.

Travis turned to face Eldrige and said evenly. "No Eldrige, those were all over done." He paused, "But I think I saw one of your alligators running toward The River."

Everyone laughed uncomfortably.

Eldrige volunteered, 'I'm sorry, Travis. The Lord gives and the Lord takes away."

"He certainly does Eldrige, he certainly does."

"Glad we were there to help," Tom said, patting Travis on the shoulder.

"Mom, how about some music?"

Katherine hurried to the house and returned with a radio.

Morgan sat down next to Travis. Carolina, sensing the men's need to talk, rose from the table. Tom sat down and Eldrige sat next to him.

Tom said, "I talked to the Fire Marshal today. He said that the fire was started from a cigarette. They traced the call, but it seems that the caller was not the one who started it. Maybe the guy who did it didn't even know what he'd done."

"Edication don't modify idjits, my daddy used to say."

"Spoken for true, Eldrige," Travis replied. "The power company said there was a fried night owl on the ground by the blown power pole. I guess he straddled the wires and shorted it."

"There's no end to the problems that come up," Carl offered.

"My pastures are getting mighty dry, too. I don't know whether to sell off the heifers who need more feed, or keep them and cull the older cows," Eldrige said.

"I have the same problem, Eldrige. It won't take long before we have more in them than they're worth. What are you going to do, Morgan?" Everyone looked at him, waiting for the answer.

"I have fields lined up to put some of them on, but they won't be ready until frost. It seems like it's always your time or money. I guess I'll cull the older cows and put the money into growing out the young ones. I'll have to pull the calves early if I use the wheat fields for the heifers. It's a hard call."

Carl nodded. "It looks like a dry winter."

"I'm going to move most of what I have left into the east pasture. I don't really need to cull any more right now. I already sold a bunch," Travis said wryly.

Morgan reached up and put his hand on Travis's shoulder, giving it a hard squeeze before roughly shoving it away.

"Well, it's one day closer to rain," Tom said.

"I guess the six-inch rain we had last month was our rainy season. It sure didn't help much."

"Right again, Eldrige," Tom answered. "When the drops are six inches apart it don't wet much. There's nothing left of spring but the weeds."

"This land sets its seasons by the rain. I guess we're only going to have one season this year," Travis said.

"My dirt tanks are going dry," Tom added. "I hope the wind keeps turning the windmills or there won't be enough water for the cattle. The grass in the wheelhouse pasture is burnt up. I had to move them. I guess some of them are going to the sale soon."

"The cracks in the pastures are so big that the calves are falling in. Even the grasshoppers won't eat the grass, it's so dry. The cows are starting to give powdered milk," Eldrige said.

The men fell silent, nodding in agreement. The lean times weren't funny anymore.

The crowd began to disperse. Thanking Katherine and Travis for the meal, they trailed to their vehicles with full and sleepy children slung over shoulders. Mother and son began to gather up the leftover food.

Carolina said, "Here, let me help, Katherine."

"No. No. You and Travis take a walk. Morgan and I will clean up. Won't we, Morgan?"

Morgan nodded and picked up a trash barrel to finish cleaning off the tables. "Go ahead, girl. Katherine and I will get this and then have a cup of coffee. If I decide to leave, Travis can bring you home, right, Travis?"

"Yes, sir. Come on Carolina, let's take a walk."

She fell in step with him, and they walked towards the corrals.

"That sure was a good meal, Travis. You did that beef just right."

"Yep. I got a good scald on it as my daddy used to say."

"You did, indeed. How are the girls handling the fire?"

"They're doing fine but we have to keep a close eye on them. All those critters that lost their homes are in the home pasture."

"What do you mean?"

"There's been a lot of snakes, scorpions, spiders and such. A bunch of the mice got in the barn, and a family of skunks. The girls are upset with me because we won't let them out of the house unless Mom or I are with them."

"Poor things. That's hard. But they know how to look out for spiders and skunks."

"I have enough to worry about without having to worry about that," he snapped.

"I'm sorry, Travis. I know. What a lot you are going through."

"I have some fence down. I lost at least three sections of grass. Although that might not be too bad since it was dried up, anyway. I haven't talked to the insurance man to see what's covered. Probably nothing."

Not knowing what to say, she slipped her arm through his and pressed it close to her side.

They continued past the corrals and started towards the pasture.

"Travis, how many head did you lose?"

"Carolina, I don't want to talk about it anymore."

She stopped and turned to face him. He slid an arm around her and pulled her to him, kissing her fiercely.

He grasped Carolina by her shoulders, pushed her away and said, "I'm sorry. I'm not very good company right now. I think I'm going crazy. We better get back."

Chapter 21
Denver
1865

Morgan drove the wagon to the train station and waited as Mr. Randel dismounted. He handed down his boss's suitcase and turned the team to the livery stable. Sophia was seated on a bench in the Ticketmaster's office. When she waved slightly, he touched his hat. After leaving instructions with the livery man, Morgan shouldered his worn army haversack and walked through the dusty street toward the train station.

He watched the passengers mounting the steps to the coaches and saw his boss and Sophia's father looking around, apparently waiting for him. He stepped into the newspaper office to purchase a paper and stood, perusing the headlines. *If the porters don't do it, let the old farts handle the baggage themselves. Randel wants to court my girl, let him work for it. I'm not going to help him look good.*

Morgan noticed the time on the station clock and strolled along the street, ignoring the waves of the men, until he reached the train. All eyes were upon him. He looked directly at Mr. Randel and said, "Oh, I'm sorry. Did everyone need my help? Let me get these bags."

He ignored the glares of the men and the slight smile on Sophia's lips as he gathered the bags and waited as the two men and Sophia mounted the steps to the traveling coach.

A black, uniformed porter appeared and reached for the bags. His badge read Brotherhood of Sleeping Car Porters. "Sorry sir, we's running a little late gettin' everythin' loaded. I'll get these to the sleepin' car, beggin' yo pardon."

Morgan nodded and followed the men and Sophia up the steps. He took a seat behind and across from the trio, affording him a good view of his love. He rubbed his hand over the oxblood velvet on the horsehair seat as he sat ramrod straight with face composed, revealing nothing of the turmoil inside. Without looking up, he opened the newspaper and began to read, occasionally looking over the top of the paper to find her covertly watching him.

A request of the porter produced a card table and a deck of playing cards. The three began a game of Fan Tan. As the cards were laid out, domino style, Morgan could follow the game and the conversation. Plans for shopping in the stores, a visit to the Jenny Lind Theatre, anticipated meals, the Denver House where they were all staying.

Morgan studied Sophia. Her reseda jacquard dress was trimmed in black passementerie. Her deep auburn hair was caught in a beaded snood at the base of her neck. A matching beaded reticule lay in her lap. The black patent leather shoes, peaking from under the hem of her skirt, were closed with pearl gray buttons. He ached to hold her. *I better get my mind off of her or I won't make it to Denver.*

Morgan examined the cabin. The dark walnut paneling was carved in filigree patterns where it coved to meet the stamped copper ceiling tiles. He studied the garden scene on the curtains before pulling them back and tying them with the braided cord that hung from the brass hooks. He glanced at Sophia as he turned to watch the landscape flying by, disappointed that she was deeply intent on the card game. Morgan dozed and when he woke, his three traveling companions had retired to their private rooms, leaving him to sleep in the available space. He untied the gold cords and let the curtains fall together. Pulling off his boots, he put his feet up on the upholstered seat across from him and, using his haversack for a pillow, settled in for the night.

The soft morning light from the opaque windows overhead filled the cabin. Morgan woke and stared at the colors dancing on the ceiling, a reflection from the crystals which adorned the overhead lamps. He lay still and listened to the steady click of the wheels on the rails while he oriented himself to the day, then reached up to tie back the curtains. The grassy plains had given way to timber and mountains. The air in the cabin was much cooler. It smelled green, not the brown dusty air around Dickson. He pulled his jacket from the bag and went to find a place to wash up.

I wonder where she's sleeping. He passed an unoccupied berth and stopped to take in the sight. A burled walnut dresser with a carved white marble top sat against one wall. The matching framed mirror reflected a curled brass bed with an embroidered coverlet and matching pillow.

He turned quickly and hurried to the washroom at the end of the car, embarrassed and troubled by thoughts of Sophia. The vision of her in that bed, sleeping with her auburn hair spread across that pillow aroused in him a deep, aching hunger.

Ablutions completed, he returned to his seat and sat studying the landscape, waiting for his fellow travelers to emerge.

"Say, there. My name is Carter. On my way to Denver. I sell haberdashery and men's clothing items." The dapper young man stuck out his hand.

"My name's Donnally. I'm with my boss going to Denver to purchase some horses."

"Ah ha! May I sit down here? Thank you. You wouldn't be with the two gentlemen and the lovely young lady who were in here yesterday, would you?"

"I would," Morgan replied, annoyed at the mention of Sophia.

"A comely lass, indeed."

"Indeed. And spoken for."

"Oh! Well! Do you have need of any accouterments for yourself?"

"No. I'm fine, thank you."

"Well, very good then."

The man sat silent, studying his hands, then said, "Minding my manners, Lieutenant, might I say that the Kepi you wear appears to be from the South? Sir, I don't mean to offend but I would offer you a word of caution. This is northern country. You might find it advantageous to view my wares. I have, in one of my cases, a couple of hats that you might want to consider."

Morgan looked at the eager young man, pondering his words. "I guess it wouldn't hurt to look."

"Fine. Fine. Why don't you join me in my cabin, and I'll open my cases for you? I also have catalogs from which you may order."

Morgan rose and indicated that he would follow the man.

The salesman eagerly opened a large leather case with several hats stacked inside and handed one of them to Morgan. He fitted it on his head and examined himself in the tiny mirror which Carter held before him. Indicating a negative opinion, Morgan handed it back.

"I have a nice brown derby here," the man said, holding up a hat for Morgan to see. Morgan shook his head. "Then you probably are not interested in this pork pie?"

Again, Morgan shook his head, indicating that he did not like that one. *I can't stand anything pork!* he thought to himself.

The salesman offered him a picture brochure. "This is a new company. The hatter is John Batterson Stetson. He has opened a small enterprise in Philadelphia offering felted beaver hats. Available in natural, gray, or black. Four-inch brim and crown. Waterproof. A sweat band on the inside and a hat band to adjust the size to your own head. An excellent hat for a discerning man such as yourself who is out in the weather."

Pausing to take a breath and ignoring Morgan's shaking head, he continued, "It may take a month or so to get it delivered to you. May I say that I think you would look mighty fine in one of these."

He indicated a picture in the brochure. "It's called The Boss of the Plains. I'm taking orders because Mr. Stetson won't send less than a dozen at a time. I have three orders already. Six dollars, in advance."

"I don't plan on being around in a month. What do you have for sale right now?"

In a less enthusiastic tone the persistent man said, "This here is a nice slouch hat. It only comes in black. Very reasonable," and handed Morgan a wide-brimmed wool felt hat.

Morgan tried it on and studied himself in the mirror. Leaving it on his head he asked, "How much for this one?"

"That is an excellent choice, sir. Wide brim, felted wool, sheds water, air pocket to keep your head cool."

"How much?"

"Two dollars now and it is yours."

"How about six bits right now. It isn't new."

"You are a hard man, Mr. Donnally. I will, however, accept your offer since, as you have pointed out, it has been fitted to many heads. "Could I help you find something else to complete your ensemble?"

"No. I'm finished."

Morgan rose and fished in his pocket for the coins.

"I thank you for your patronage and hope that you will take my card. Perhaps, we can do more business in the future."

He exchanged the coins for the man's card and shook his hand. "Thank you, Mr. Carter."

Morgan took his time shaping the crown to suit himself, settled the new hat on his head and returned to the traveling car.

Sophia raised her head and a look of delight danced across her face when she saw Morgan in his new hat.

The men, noticing her look, turned quickly to see what she had spied. Seeing Morgan, they both frowned and turned around, engaging Sophia in conversation, drawing her attention away from the hired hand. Morgan tucked the gray Kepi in his haversack and sat down, rearranging the new hat to fit his head.

The train eased into a station and came to a halt. The porter walked through the car and announced, "Ladies and gentlemen, we will be reaching Denver in about two hours. This is a water stop. Soon there will be some boys boarding with sandwiches, and drinks. They may have some apples, cheese, and such. Feel free to purchase or you may debark and partake of the fine fare at the nearby Harvey House. We will depart in one hour."

Morgan watched as Sophia rose and, escorted by the two men, left the car without looking back. Fighting down the jealousy which rose in him, he called to mind their last conversation and dwelt on her promise, calming his anxious heart.

Morgan indicated to the scrawny boy standing before him that he would take a sandwich and a Mason jar of tea. "I'll be back in a few minutes for the jar, sir."

Morgan nodded and stared out of the window, straining to catch a glimpse of Sophia.

The passengers reappeared after the meal and Morgan avoided the curious looks by reading the paper left by the newsboy who came through the cars hawking the Denver News.

Mr. Randel appeared in front of Morgan blocking his view. "Morgan, when we get to Denver, take the transport to the hotel with the baggage. You will stay at the Denver Hotel with us. The rooms have been arranged. You can take the rest of the day off. See the sights, do any shopping or anything else you've a mind to. Eat when you want. Charge it to the room."

"Yes sir. Thank you." *He's letting me know my place. And keeping me away from Sophia.*

"We will meet in front of the hotel tomorrow at six thirty and catch a transport to the parade grounds. There will be food over there, but we want to have time to look over the stock before the bidding starts."

"I'll be there in the morning, Mr. Randel."

"Nice hat, by the way."

Morgan glared at the man's back as he turned to rejoin Sophia at the table.

Morgan woke early the next morning and prepared to meet his boss in front of the hotel.

"Good morning, Morgan."

"Good morning, Mr. Randel. Good day for a sale."

"Yes, it is. Good morning, Chatham," Randel said, turning his back on Morgan.

The hotel transport arrived, the men entered, and found places among the other men riding to the sale.

"It looks like they might have run some ringers in, Mr. Randel. These are not all cavalry horses."

"I can see that, Morgan. Check for lungers and such things. We need horses that have the stamina to work stock."

The men walked among the horses, each commenting while Mr. Randel took notes.

"This black has wide eyes and nice slope to the shoulder. Straight legs. Good feet. Number 197."

"How about this one, Morgan?"

"He looks good except that he's slightly ewe necked. He might have breathing problems if he's worked too hard."

"You are a keen observer of horseflesh, Morgan."

"Thank you, sir. I haven't seen any CSA brands. President Davis handpicked a lot of his officers from the West Point graduates. They received the best firearms and the finest horses. I wish we could find some of those."

"Did you sell any horses to him before you got burned out?'

"Yes, we did. My father and I bred some of the best horses in Tennessee. Not bragging, sir. My father was an excellent judge of horses. We had some great stallions."

Morgan's keen eye for equine excellence continued to serve. "This one isn't a cavalry horse, Number 211. He looks Spanish. He has good muscle on his back. It looks like he has one less vertebra. His back is a little shorter."

"He won't travel smooth, Morgan."

"No, sir, but he'll have stamina for hard work."

"He looks tough, all right."

"Number 93. Good neck, eyes wide and clear, straight legs."

"Number 14 looks good, but the high withers mean he'll need a special saddle. Otherwise, he'll get sore early on."

"I don't want to buy a special saddle for one horse."

"My thoughts exactly, sir, but we might want to see if there are any general saddles for high and low withers, short back and such. Just having two or three extra saddles might make a difference in how the remuda performs all day."

"Probably mostly McClellans here, not working saddles," Randel remarked.

"Maybe so," Morgan said, noting his boss's growing irritation.

"When we finish looking these over, we can take a gander at the equipment before the sale starts, but any of those horses will have to be exceptional."

"Understood."

"Morgan, we have about twenty to bid on. That's enough. We only need about ten for the ranch." They started walking towards the auction arena. Morgan took a deep breath and glanced at his boss.

He said, "Mr. Randel, sir, I was wondering if you would allow me to purchase two horses for myself and run them on the range."

Randel stopped and turned to face Morgan. "Why do you want to do that? The horses that I purchase are for you and the men. You can have first choice."

"I appreciate that, sir, but I would like to be able to work on them when I have time and maybe sell them on my own. Make a little extra money."

Randel was slow to answer as he studied his hired hand. "Morgan, I wouldn't mind that so much but if I let you do it then the rest of the men will want to do the same, or maybe put cows on my range. Can you see where that might lead?"

A hardness formed in Morgan's stomach, and he forced out the words. "Yes, I can see how that might be difficult for you."

"Come join Mr. Chatham and myself for a bite to eat. The bidding starts at one."

The sale over and arrangements made for transportation left Morgan with nothing to do. He could hear the laughter from the lobby as people gathered for the evening. Morgan sat, staring morosely into his drink. He had stationed himself at the bar, facing the open doors, hoping to get a glimpse of her.

He looked up when he heard familiar voices and saw Sophia walking between the two men. She had changed into a rose satin gown with the fashionable Garabaldi sleeves, trimmed in gold braid. Her black woven wrap was draped loosely around her bare shoulders. She did not look around the room as she was escorted to the front door. Sophia had placed a bit of greenery in her upswept hair. He smiled when he realized that it was a sprig of lavender. *You say so little and yet so much, my love.*

Morgan selected the same seat that Sophia had occupied just three days before. He inhaled deeply but the only thing he detected was the scent of worn leather and the sour smell of many travelers. The sound of the clicking wheels on the track lulled him into a fitful sleep, into dreams of her. Jealous dreams woke him with a start, as he swung his arm to punch Randel in the face.

He sat, with his arms locked across his chest, staring at the rushing scenery. His mind racing in time to the clickity clack of the train, searching for answers to his dilemma. *How am I going to be able to offer Sophia what she wants? Deserves?*

"Next stop, Dickson," the porter announced, jarring Morgan out of his reverie.

He tipped his hat to block the afternoon sun from burning into his eyes as he stepped down and headed for the livestock cars. He watched as the conductor directed the engine to pull forward and stop at the raised chute while each car was unloaded. He looked around when he heard his name called.

Zeke and Corky were riding towards the pens, followed by Parnell, who had picked up the buckboard at the livery. Two saddled mounts were tied to the tail gate. Parnell waved at Morgan. He lifted his hand in salute and returned to the study of the disembarking of the horses which were in his charge. He stepped forward, signed the receiving papers, and handed them to Parnell.

"I don't think they're going to let us leave them in the corral for long. I ate on the train. I'm ready when you are."

"Then let's get them lined out and headed home."

Morgan stepped into the corral, lariat in hand, and moved slowly among the horses. He cut each one of those destined for the Rafter R from the churning herd and began moving each of them to the gate. With a nod to Corky, who opened the gate, Morgan drove the first horse through. He moved to the next and the next until eight horses had been cut from those milling around the pen.

"Parnell, we have some saddles and freight in the box car ahead. We should load them in the wagon, don't you think?"

Parnell nodded and pulled the wagon up beside the railroad car. He waited while Morgan showed his papers and retrieved the saddles and boxes.

"Mr. Randel wired me to bring your gear, so I brought your horse."

Morgan nodded. 'That suits me."

"Let's head 'em out."

The men worked to keep the horses gathered up and moving in the right direction. Nothing was said beyond the whooping that the men maintained, driving the horses along the dusty road.

Morgan was relieved to see headquarters as the afternoon sun melted into the gray October haze.

Penning the new arrivals, the men unsaddled and turned their mounts in with the other horses. They all leaned on the rails to study the newly purchased horses and watch as they squealed and bit each other, kicking, establishing a new pecking order among the herd.

"Well, men, Cookie said he would have supper hot for us when we got back. Let's go get it." Parnell slapped Morgan on his back and said, "I bet you missed the old lady's cooking, now didn't you, Morgan."

"I'm surprised but, yes, I did. I like the way he burns a steak."

The men were laughing as they entered the cook shack.

"Glad you're back, Morgan. What'd you see in Denver? Any purty dancing girls?" Cookie asked.

"No, but I saw lots of horses. Miss Sophia helped Mr. Randel purchase some spices and utensils for you. We have some new dishes and cutlery for the house. The boxes are still in the wagon. We should unload them."

"Whoo hoo. She's going to civilize all of us. I bet we get new curtains next," Zeke said.

"She probably don't want to look in and see us in our Union suits," Corky chimed in.

"If'n she's here at the ranch, I don't think she'll be looking in our window."

"Shut the hell up, you two. That's no way to talk about a lady," Morgan rose, and glaring at the men, strode quickly into the night.

"What's up with him? I didn't mean nothin' by it."

"Mr. Randel is courting her, so watch your mouth," Parnell warned.

"Hey! Mr. Randel is back," Corky hollered into the barn. Zeke put down the bellows and Morgan dropped the horseshoe into a bucket of water. The men gathered around the buckboard and greeted the boss.

"Good morning, Mr. Randel. How was your trip?"

"It was fine, Parnell. How's everything here?"

"Just fine. The boys are shoeing the last of the horses. Morgan has worked a few of them. Some fine stock you bought, sir."

"Good. Good. Everything else all right around here?"

"Yes, sir."

"Son of a bitch!" Zeke yelled, jumping around on one boot. He kicked the other one off and turned it upside down. A rock bounced and clattered across the floor. Morgan chortled and Corky bent over laughing, slapping his knees.

"Got you that time, Zeke," Corky crowed.

"You ignert son of a bitch! I'm gonna kill you. I like to have a heart attack."

Zeke started towards Corky, Morgan stepped between them.

"Zeke I sure do understand the sentiment, but Mr. Randel won't take kindly to you killing the help. Especially since we need to start gathering cattle."

Zeke stood, fists clenched, looking from Morgan to Corky. "You'll probably live forever, you ignert peckerwood. The Lord don't want you and the devil won't take you."

"I surely do hope that's not true, Zeke. About the Lord, that is," said Corky, suddenly contrite.

The angry man pushed past Morgan and charged through the door, heading for the cook shack.

Morgan fell in beside Corky and said, "Lighten up, old man, or you're going to get your lamp trimmed."

Corky nodded.

Breakfast was silent until Parnell showed up. "Good morning, men. After breakfast I want you to split up and start looking for cattle. We will gather three hundred head and put them on the flats. Corky, you ride far north and Zeke, you start west. I'll push from the south. Morgan, I want you to ride east. Be sure to get into the cane and under the trees along The River. They like to shade up in there."

The men nodded.

Mr. Randel entered the cook shack.

"Good morning, men." Cookie rose and handed him a cup of coffee. Randel sat down in the vacated chair.

"Day after tomorrow you start for Fort Sumner with the herd. Get yourselves gathered up. Cookie will be along in the wagon. It should take about eleven days up and maybe nine coming back. Don't want to walk the tallow off the cattle. Any questions?"

He looked at each of the men. "Apparently not. Make sure you get the count rounded up by this evening, so we don't have to spend a lot of time looking for them tomorrow. Don't get the young cows or calves. We'll gather and work them when you get back. See you in the morning."

Randel rose and left. The men looked at each other and then at Parnell.

"Somebody needs to stay at the ranch to look after things. I think Morgan would be the best bet for that. Mr. Randel will be here if you have any questions, Morgan. Any objections?" he asked, turning to Morgan.

"Nope."

Morgan helped Cookie load and pull a canvas tarp over the supplies in the wagon while the rest of the men saddled up. Parnell gave a wave of his hand and the men, followed by the wagon, were soon out of sight.

"Well, Morgan, it's just you and me for a while. Do what you normally do but don't wander too far from the headquarters," said Randel.

"Yes, sir. I'll work on those horses we got in Denver."

Sophia set a plate of eggs in front of her father and another across from him. "What are you going to do about that letter, Father?" she asked as she slid into a chair.

"I think I'm going to take them up on their offer," he said, silently rereading the letter from the nominating committee. "Wouldn't you like to be a Senator's daughter? We would spend part of each year in Santa Fe. Of course, I don't know what Randel is going to say about this. He might not want you that far away."

"It doesn't matter what he wants. I haven't said I would marry him. Only think about it. He's trying to crowd me."

"Sophia, if you really are not interested in him, you can probably find someone in Santa Fe who suits you, but I wish you would consider Randel. I better send one of the men with a note for him. You can go with us when we meet for the nomination."

"I'll stay here. I can watch the place while you're gone. The cowboys will take care of anything that goes wrong."

"You are just like your mother," he said, shaking his head. "I know when I can't turn you around, but you are not going to stay out here alone. You'll go to town. You can stay with friends. If you don't want that, you can stay at the hotel. That is my final offer, Sophia. I'm leaving on Monday. I'll be back on Saturday."

She nodded and smiled at him, wondering how she could get word to Morgan.

Morgan was sitting at the table when Randel walked into the cook shack. "Morning, Morgan." He greeted the boss and continued eating.

Randel poured a cup of coffee and sat down, studying his hired hand. He pushed a piece of paper across the table. Morgan unfolded it and read. "The bearer of this may charge anything within reason to the account of David Randel. Rafter R Ranch."

Morgan nodded and slipped it in his pocket.

"Chatham and I are going to Santa Fe for about a week. Maybe more. You'll have to look after things."

"Will do." Morgan said. "Will Miss Chatham be going with you?"

Randel looked sharply at Morgan before answering. "No."

"I just wondered if she needed looking after."

"She'll be in town. Where she's safe. She won't need looking after."

"Yes, sir. I'll look after things here."

"Good." his boss said in a hard tone.

Two days of biscuits and gravy. Flour and canned milk were the only things left behind when Cookie loaded the wagon for Fort Sumner. Morgan looked balefully at the plate and started poking around in the cabinets for something to stretch out the meager fare. Four days out and the larder was bare.

"We're getting low on grub, Lieutenant. I guess we need to make a foray into town," Morgan said out loud to himself, recalling the victuals that he survived on in the army.

Morgan cleaned up his plate and wiped the pan clean. He found a tow sack and saddled his dun.

Pulling up at the livery he said to the old cowboy who appeared, "I don't need anything but a place to corral the horse for a few hours."

The toothless old man nodded and reached for the reins. "I got 'em."

Morgan stepped into the General Store and began selecting canned goods. Tomatoes, peaches, canned meat. He picked up a can of salmon, studied it, and put it back on the shelf. He set his selections on the counter, in front of the clerk. "Would you put this on Mr. Randel's account. Rafter R."

"I've never seen you in here before. Where's the usual man?"

"Cookie is on a trail drive to Fort Sumner. He didn't fill the larder before he left. I can show you the chit if you need it."

"I do."

Morgan pulled the paper from his vest and watched as the man studied it. Putting it back in his pocket, he continued placing cans on the counter. The man silently wrote the sums in a ledger and filled the tow sack with the canned goods.

"Thank you for your business, sir," the man said stiffly as he handed the sack to Morgan.

"You're welcome."

Sophia stepped out into the sunlight and shaded her eyes against the morning sun. *I wonder if I can get by with renting a horse or buggy.* She started across the street to the livery, looking around to be sure that no one that she knew had seen her.

Morgan saw her as she stood talking to the livery man and hurried down the street.

"Why, Miss Chatham. What a pleasure to see you. Are you going for a drive?" He tipped his hat.

"I was just inquiring about a runabout."

"Why don't you let me help you. A lady shouldn't go around by herself. Where's your father?"

"He's away on business, Mr. Donnally."

"Let me store this grub while he gets the horse harnessed. I'll take you wherever you want to go."

"Thank you, Mr. Donnally."

Morgan assisted her into the rig and walked around to the other side. They sat on each side of the buggy until they were out of sight of the town.

"I was on my way out to see you, Morgan."

"I'm glad that I was already in town."

He reached for her, and she slid close to him, raising her face for his kiss.

"Father has been asked to take the nomination for State Senator. He and David have gone to Santa Fe. Father wanted me to go with him. I said 'no' so he told me to stay at the hotel until he gets back."

"I sure am glad you did, Sophia. It gives us some time together."

Sophia tucked her arm in his and snuggled against him. "Have you thought of anything, Morgan?"

"I've been thinking about going back to Tennessee to see if there is anything left that I can sell. I have an uncle back there."

"Morgan, I have some savings. Not much but maybe I could go with you to Tennessee."

"Thank you, my dear, but I can't ask you to do that. You're better off staying with your father until I get this worked out. I want to do this the right way. Mr. Randel won't let me run any horses on his range. I don't blame him, but it would have been a way to get some extra money."

He turned to look at her, tucking a loose tendril of auburn hair behind her ear. He stopped the buggy, wrapped an arm tightly around her shoulders and kissed her. Picking up the reins, he urged the horse on.

She laid her hand lightly on his knee and he covered it with his, squeezing her fingers.

"Father is pushing me to accept David. He's been coming to the house more than usual. He's buying things for his house, asking for my opinion and such. Father keeps bringing it up. I don't know what to do about that."

"Tell them both that you're not ready to make such a serious commitment and you want to think about it without feeling pressed for a decision. Threaten to go back east for some more education. That should make them back off. Don't lead him on, Sophia, That's not right."

She moved her hand and rested it on his thigh. He lost his train of thought as the heat of her touch burned through his gray woolen pants. Morgan laid his hand on hers, lacing their fingers together.

"Do you love me, Morgan?"

"Since the first day I saw you. Let's stop and walk for a while, my love."

She nodded. He pulled up and stepped down. Morgan lifted her from the wagon. She slid her hand around his neck, drew him close and pressed against him as she slid to the ground. He pulled her hair until her face was tilted up to his. He studied it before kissing her deep and long. She sighed.

Grasping her hand, Morgan started walking, leading the horse.

"I've thought about trying a hand in the Colorado gold fields, but I think they're played out. I thought about joining the Federal army, but I don't think I could deal with that, and we'd be apart again."

"We could homestead, Morgan. There's still land available further west."

"I'm no farmer, Sophia. I know horses and cattle. There are a lot of stories of people starving out on those parcels."

He stopped and wrapped his arms around her, aching for more. "Sophia, I don't want to be away from you anymore. Those war years were enough to last a lifetime."

She ran her hands up and down his back with her face pressed into his chest. He shivered. *She wants to know how I feel. She wants me as much as I want her.*

"Let's get back into the buggy, Sophia." He lifted her up and followed, urging the horse forward. "Sophia, I've tried to come up with something, but nothing has worked out yet. We have to start gathering cattle when Mr. Randel gets back. It'll take several days. The cows are starting to calve, and we need to move them. They're scattered to hell and gone... Excuse me. They're everywhere. They're moving because of the cats."

"Father said the same thing. The cowboys are supposed to help work David's cattle. The River is running full with the runoff." Sophia turned to face him, a note of concern in her voice. She reached up and touched his cheek.

"Morgan, be very careful. A few years back he lost a hired hand, Charlie Dunn. Everyone thinks that he got caught in The River. It's dangerous."

He slid an arm around her, pulling her close to him, touched by her concern.

"I guess we should head back. We only have about an hour of daylight."

"We can have supper in one of the private dining rooms at the hotel."

"I'm not sure that's a good idea, Sophia."

"Of course, it is. We won't eat in the main dining room."

"It's hard to resist you, my love." Sophia slid a decorous distance from him as the town came into sight and changed the conversation, smiling.

"That was a great supper, Sophia. I guess I should be going." Morgan stood and reached into his pocket for money.

"I can charge this to my room. You don't need to pay."

"No, that isn't right, and we don't need to leave any tracks."

Sophia nodded, understanding. "Please walk me to my room, Morgan."

"I'm not sure I should do that."

"Do you want me walking alone through this hotel?"

"Sophia..." Morgan started to speak and then looked into her upturned face. Her eyes were dark and smoldering. He had never seen her like this before. Nervously, he pulled her chair back as she rose. They walked together up the stairs to her room, their shoulders touching, silent. She handed him the key and he reached around her to unlock the door. "Come in," she whispered.

"I better not. It's not fitting."

"Morgan, it isn't fitting for us to be standing in this hallway. Come in," she said, reaching for his hand.

"It isn't proper, I better go."

"Morgan, please come in. I have something I want to show you." Her voice, warm and liquid, poured over him. Her eyes beckoning.

He slowly entered the room and removed his hat, rolling it in his hands as he looked around at the damask coverlet with matching pillows piled against the walnut headboard. *Like the room on the train.* His heart began to race. A matching wardrobe and cheval mirror stood against one wall. Her leather satchel sat open on a fiddleback chair in front of a walnut writing table with an oxblood leather top. The scent of lavender filled the room. Her scent. He could hear his heart pounding as he watched her remove a small brown satin covered box from her bag.

"Do you know what this is?" she asked, opening it and holding it in front of him. He could barely hear her for the blood rushing in his ears.

Looking from the open box to her eyes he said hoarsely, "I believe I do. It's called a French Shield. Where did you get it?"

She laughed at his discomfiture. "I went to Miss Potter's school for young ladies. Girls have lots of time before the lights go out. We read <u>Fruits of Philosophy</u> to each other and looked through women's magazines."

"Why do you have this, Sophia?" He asked sternly, concerned that he did not know her very well.

"It was a schoolgirl lark, Morgan. The girls I boarded with decided that we would each order one. As you can see, I have never opened mine." She held it up for inspection.

The flame rose from his chest to his hairline. He reached up and rubbed his forehead as he looked away.

"Sophia, I better go. Now."

She moved closer to him and slid her arms around him, pressing her face into his chest.

"I'm sorry. I didn't mean to embarrass you. We are pledged to each other, are we not? I wanted this to be a special time. For us."

He could feel her hot breath through his shirt. "I have waited years for this, Sophia. I can only stand so much."

His arms wrapped around her, crushing her to him. Trepidation melted as he kissed her hard, seeking. He undid her linen shirtwaist with slow deliberateness, hands trembling, controlling his urge to rip it from her. His large fingers clumsily undid the tiny buttons. She had filled his thoughts and dreams for so long that the reality was unbearable.

He watched as she undid and stepped out of her skirt and stood before him in her lace trimmed chemise. He undid the ribbon lacing and slipped the undergarment slowly from her shoulders. It dropped to the floor. He ran his fingers along her collar bone and kissed her bare shoulders. The scent of her had filled his dreams, coming as it had in every letter she sent. The fragrance of lavender forever a reminder of her.

He curled his arms around her and carried her to the bed, kneeling on the coverlet as he laid her down, propped against the pillows. Morgan quickly removed his own clothes as he gazed at the beauty of her. He pulled off her shoes and slowly moved his hand up her leg as he laid down beside her. He began stroking her, kissing her warm skin gently, arousing a need in her. She clung to him. His lips traced her collarbone to the small indentation of her throat.

"I have wanted to do this since the first day I saw you," he whispered.

His hands explored her, learning everything about her, drinking in the scent and warmth of her, filling his senses with the memories.

They lay together, spent. The silence blossoming into conversation then fading back into silent thoughts until they couldn't tell what had been thought and what had been spoken.

Chapter 22
The Metal Detector
2012

Carolina was preparing lesson plans when the phone rang. "Donnally residence."

"Hello, Carolina. How you doin'?" Travis said, cheerfully.

"Just fine. We haven't heard from you in weeks, Travis. Where have you been?"

"Putting up fence, mostly."

"That must have been hard with the wind blowing like it has."

"You're right about that. It's been blowing so hard that it kept blowing me back to the day before. I like to never got it done."

Surprised at his tone, she laughed. *Back to normal, finally.*

"That wind just keeps blowing. You'd think that it would finally run out, but it seldom does."

"My Dad calls it the eternal, infernal wind."

"Good name for it. That's how we get this good topsoil around here. Well anyway, the reason I called is this. I'm going to take the day off. Mom bought me a metal detector and I've already asked Morgan if I can scout around the old homestead in his west pasture. I was wondering if you might want to go with me. We have leftovers from supper, and I thought I would pack us a basket of chicken and things. Mom said she would take care of the girls. We can make a day of it. What do you say?"

"I say that I would like that a lot."

Carolina turned on the radio. Travis drove slowly, studying the dried-up pastures. A dust devil danced across the dry ground, teasing the Sacaton. A group of cows approached a small clump of trees, looking for shade, and a flock of blackbirds fell like autumn leaves to the earth, searching for something to eat. Everything had gone underground, escaping the unseasonable fall temperatures.

The morning sun was already causing a glare on the windows, radiating into the cab of the truck. A robin stood in the shadow of a fence post, wings outspread, mouth open, suffering in the heat. Even in the early morning, the sky was fading, bleached by the sun. The air had lost the green growing scent and smelled old, dried up, lifeless.

They pulled up in front of an old adobe house. The wooden door swung on one hinge, exposing the dark interior. As they opened the truck doors, they looked down, checking for snakes.

"Dad always warned me about this place. It's kind of creepy."

"He told me that this was probably one of the first homesteads in the area."

"Right. He only brought me here one time when I was about ten and warned me against this place and the horseshoe bend in The River."

"That's why I thought we might find something," Travis said as he pulled the metal detector from the back of the truck. "Maybe some buried money or something."

"A treasure hunt. Yay. It's been a long time since we've been on a treasure hunt. I can't help thinking that someone's dreams have died when I see an old homestead like this."

"Or maybe they moved on to something better."

"Yes. Let's think good thoughts."

Even at the end of summer the heat pulled the moisture from her skin. She watched Travis studying her mouth as she pulled a lip balm from her pocket and smoothed it over her lips. He unconsciously licked his lips. "Do you want some," she asked, offering the tube. He grinned and she said, "I meant the lip balm."

"No thanks, I'm fine." He gestured to the sky. "Look at the buzzard migration. I guess they should have my pasture cleaned up in no time."

"Travis," she cautioned.

"You're right. None of that today."

She started for the door of the old building. He blocked her with an arm and said, "Wait a minute."

He pulled a shovel from the bed of the truck. "We need to be armed for critters."

They stepped cautiously forward and peered into the shadows. Broken furniture and the acrid smell of rodents clouded the air as the animals scurried to escape the intruders.

"Do you think there's anything in here?"

"I doubt it. Somebody would have found it by now. We will probably be better off looking around outside. Where would you hide money if you lived here, Carolina?"

"I think I would start around the well. It would be a marker that would stay here for a long time. Not too far from the house.

"Good choice," Travis said, assembling the metal detector.

"That's a pretty fancy metal detector, Travis."

"Mom gave it to me for my birthday. She said that I needed to do something besides worry about the ranch. She and Dad used to hunt arrow heads and scout old homesteads."

"I remember when we were kids and went exploring. Those were good times."

"Yep."

"I forgot how much fun we used to have," he said, examining a bridle bit.

Carolina studied him. He had pulled his hat down, shading his eyes. Streams of perspiration tracked through his day-old growth of beard, his shirt molded to his broad, thick shoulders, the muscles flexing under the damp cloth as he tossed the debris aside. Glistening drops of perspiration slipped down the curls that clung to his thick, muscular neck.

He straightened in time to catch her looking at him. "See something you like, Carolina?"

She blushed and turned away. 'No. I was just thinking about how we've changed and grown up. Do you do this with your girls?"

"I haven't in a long time. I guess I should have brought them along, but Mom thought that it was time for me to get away from everything, even the girls."

"I'm glad that you asked me to come with you. This is fun."

Travis pushed back his hat, exposing his glistening head. His hair fell forward in damp curls on his forehead. "Are you ready to eat, Carolina?"

"Yes," she managed to choke out.

"Let's get closer to The River, where its cooler."

"Look at that clump of trees. Aren't they apples? I wonder how they got here." Carolina pointed.

"Probably someone tossed out an apple core. Like Johnny Appleseed. See how the leaves are closed up. Like they're praying for rain."

As they approached the trees shading The River, Carolina said, "Fall must be coming soon. Not only the buzzards but the sea gulls are traveling."

Travis searched the sky and said, "They migrate to Mexico. Did you know that the seagull is the official bird of Utah?"

"I did not. You know the strangest things, Travis."

"There is much joy to be found in useless information."

"You never cease to amaze me."

"Watch me produce our lunch," he said with a flourish.

The meal finished, they cleared a place on the blanket and sat down, side by side, not touching, watching the hummingbirds dart among the salt cedar, dive bombing each other, guarding their supply of food. She imagined little fighter pilots, the soft churring belied the fierce attack of the bombardiers.

He reached for a stick and carved himself a toothpick. Want one?"

"No. I'm fine."

"Yes, you are," he said, pinching her on the hand.

"I've missed you, Travis," she said reaching to catch his hand in hers.

"Me too," he murmured, squeezing her fingers. He lay back on the blanket and looked up at her. She leaned on her elbow and stared down at him, tracing the curve of his shoulder. Slowly her fingers slid down and she tucked her fingers in his belt. Warm memories flooded through her. He silently pulled away.

"Are we starting something, Carolina?" he asked, reaching for her hand.

He sat up and looked deep into her eyes.

"I can't, Carolina. I want you so much it hurts. I could certainly do this right now, but you're still married. We are too old to just screw around like a couple of kids. We know each other too well."

"That's what makes this so easy, Travis. I forget that I'm still married when I'm with you."

"But I don't. If this is just sex it won't work for us anymore. I can't play games. If we start something, let's do it right. My girls deserve better than that. So do I. And so do you."

"I'm working on the divorce."

"Then one thing at a time."

He stood and picked up the basket.

"Well, that killed the mood. You've changed, Travis. Are we ready to go?"

"I guess so. I'm all the mes I used to be, Carolina. I'm sorry."

"Don't apologize. I just got in a mood. I shouldn't have started anything. I still love you. It's hard on me."

"I love you too, Cee. I always have, but my girls come first. My girls will measure every man by me."

"You're a good man, Travis."

"Not yet, but I'm trying. We screwed this up last time. Let's not do it again."

Carolina nodded, tears welling up in her eyes.

As they stood to go, she looked up at him with a smile that failed. He gently touched the corner of her mouth. "One thing at a time, Carolina. I want you so much right now that it's making me crazy, but if we don't do it right this time, there won't be another, agreed?"

"Agreed."

She stood in the shower and let the hot water run over her. Thoughts of Travis and their last talk, his rejection of her, tensed her muscles and clenched her soul. She turned up the hot water, trying to warm herself, trying to ease the hurt that started deep inside and went straight to her heart. She yearned for him, wanting him to hold her like he used to. She ached to dissolve into him until she was no longer a separate person. The hot water pricked her skin. She put her arms around herself, holding the memory of him close.

Carolina answered the phone.

"Hello, Darren."

"How have you been, Carolina?"

"I'm fine, Darren. Is there a reason for this call?"

"Yeah. I want to suggest a compromise. I want to see if you will let me buy out your half of the house. You have a place to live at the ranch, but I still need some place."

"Darren, you don't have any money."

"Right, but you could let me make payments. That's only right."

"No, it isn't. When this is over, I want a clean break. And I don't want any of your floozies in my house."

"When I buy you out, it won't be your house. Don't be so hard. You never used to be like this."

"I've always been like this. I don't want floozies in my house."

"Damn it, Carolina. Why are you fighting me on this? I'm trying to work out a compromise."

"If you want to go to court over this, we will. My attorney says that this is a no-fault state, and the court will divide everything we have down the middle. Except that the ranch belonged to me before we got married. I keep that. So, if you want to sell the shop, too, we can do that. Split the house and shop."

"I don't know about that."

"I do. The attorneys will get what money we have in savings. I get half of your business since we started it after we got married. The house will be sold to divide down the middle. Nobody wins."

"You win. I still don't have a place to live."

"Maybe you should have given that some thought before now."

"I'll sue for support. You make more than I do with the ranch income."

"That is off the table. The ranch is mine. My name is on the bank note for the shop. We bought it together along with the house."

"You froze our account. How am I supposed to operate?"

"You'll manage. The sooner this is over, the better for both of us."

"Damn bitch," she could hear him mutter. "I built that business by myself, without your help."

"Yes, you did. That's why I'll sign over my half to you when this is done."

"You're just handing me my ass in my hands."

"You can hardly hold your own ass in your hands when they're full of somebody else's."

"Don't start with that shit, Carolina. I'm trying to get along with you and you're being unreasonable."

"I'm through arguing with you, Darren. That is my final offer. It's either that or we go to court."

"I don't like it, Carolina. Not one damn bit, but if you're going to be unreasonable about this, I won't fight you anymore."

"You can't guilt me into anything, Darren. This is fair."

"Not by a long shot, but if you can live with yourself, I guess I can, too."

"Then we are agreed? I can tell my attorney to get the papers ready to sign?"

"I still love you, Carolina."

The vision of his parade of women ran through her mind. "I guess in your own mind you believe that you do. Darren, this is the best for both of us."

"Don't you still love me? Even a little?"

"No, Darren, I don't. Not even a little. I used to. I really did. But not anymore."

"Then this is the end of nine years of marriage."

"Yes, it is. I hope you find whatever it is that makes you happy."

"You make me happy, Carolina."

"Apparently not enough."

She listened to the silence and wondered what he was thinking.

"We are agreed then, Darren?"

"I guess so. Get the papers ready and I'll sign them."

"I'll get it done, then. Goodbye, Darren."

She tapped End Call and stood looking down at the blank screen. *As easy as that. Nine years tied in a bundle and thrown away.* She sat down and waited for the tears.

"Morgan here."

"Hi, Dad. I just wanted to tell you that it's done. Darren and I met with the lawyers and got -everything worked out. Just like you said. He keeps the business. I keep the ranch, and we sell the house. That should pay the attorneys and our bills. A fresh start for both of us."

"Glad to hear that, girl. It's for the best. I know this is hard on you. Now maybe you can think about this ranch."

"Dad, I don't want to think about that right now. I have enough to deal with."

"Carolina, I'm serious about this. Once you sign those papers, we need to have a sit down."

He hung up without any comforting words. That isn't like him. He sounded mad or something. Carolina walked through the house. The blinds were closed. The rooms looked expectant, as if they were waiting for someone to speak or laugh in the darkening gloom. She looked around the living room. The burgundy leather sofa where they slid off onto the floor while trying to make love one hot summer day. The green Aubusson rug they purchased on their vacation to New Orleans. The tables and cabinet that they ordered as their gift to each other for their third Christmas. *How happy we were to throw out the hand me downs from Darren's mother.*

The green wingbacks with the matching ottomans where they sat, side by side, watching television. *Darren wants all of these things. He can have them. I don't want the memories. Anything he leaves, I'll give to the Salvation Army. They will do someone some good.*

Carolina's phone rang. She looked at it before answering. "Hello, Dad. How are you?"

"Doing fine. When are you coming out, Carolina?" Morgan asked.

"I'm on holiday break. I have too much to do. I may get Lizbeth to come down and help me pack. The realtor is coming next week for a walk through so she can put it on Multiple Listing."

"Things are moving right along. I knew you could do it. Carolina, we still need to talk."

"Dad, can we talk on the phone? What is so important that I need to go to the ranch?" she asked, hoping against dread that everything was all right. *I don't want to have a serious conversation with Dad. I haven't even got through the divorce, yet.*

"Carolina, you need to come to the ranch. Make the time. Now would be good."

"Alright, Dad. I'll come out, now." Her heart was pounding as she packed a suitcase.

What could be so important? He almost never talks to me that way. I wonder if he's sick or something. Bad news about the ranch? Her stomach churned.

She looked around before locking the front door and walked to the mailbox. *Better get a mailbox at the post office and get my address changed.*

She placed her suitcases in the bed of the truck and slid behind the wheel. She backed to the end of the driveway and stopped to study the For Sale sign. Her hands clenched on the steering wheel. Carolina fought the mixed emotions; sadness at the end of a life she had lived for nine years, elation at the coming freedom to change, anger at Darren, shame at the failure of her marriage. The house represented all that she and Darren had planned together. *All of our dreams. It already looks abandoned and soulless.*

Carolina stepped into the small grocery and was greeted by three women, standing in a cluster.

"Why hello, Carolina. We haven't seen you in a long time. Where have you been?"

"I shop on the other side of town, mostly. I'm just picking up a few things for my dad."

"How is he, by the way?" the nearest gossip asked.

"He's just fine. Thank you for asking, Mrs. Hastings."

"Well— The reason I ask is that I saw him going into the Doctor Frank's office the other day and then Francis here saw him go into the dentist's office. Dr. Brewster. It seems like he's getting a lot of doctoring done, deary."

"I'm sure he's doing just fine, Mrs. Hastings. I would certainly be the first to know if he wasn't. It's so nice to know that you care." She forced a smile and held up her hand in a wave. *You nosy old biddies! Still, I wonder what Dad is doing.*

Carolina bought groceries before heading to the ranch, dreading the conversation that she knew her Dad had waiting for her.

"Hello, girl," Morgan said as she stepped from the truck.

"Hi, Dad." She could feel the tension. *Something was up.*

"Glad you had time to come out. I know you're busy, but the Christmas break will give you some time to get things sorted out. I want to go over things here at the ranch with you."

No introduction to this. Just dive right in. "Dad we don't call it Christmas break anymore. It's winter break."

"It might as well be called that."

Dad, are you sick?" Carolina said, picking up the bags of groceries from the back seat.

"No. What made you ask that?" Morgan reached into the bed of the truck and retrieved two suitcases.

"Well, Mrs. Hastings mentioned that she saw you going into Dr. Frank's office. and then Frances Henley saw you in Dr. Brewster's office."

"The local gossips. Don't be swayed by such things, Carolina. I'm just getting check-ups and making sure everything is all right. Just like this ranch. You and I will take a tour tomorrow so I can show you some things you need to know so you can be more hands on."

Her stomach shrank to a knot. "Sure, Dad. Tomorrow." *Hands on, uh oh.*

Carolina woke to the familiar smell of breakfast. She listened to the sound of the weather forecast on the radio as she dressed.

"Good morning, Carolina. How many eggs?"

"Just one, thanks." Everything seemed normal and yet her stomach told her that there was something wrong, different. "After we eat, I want to drive the ranch. We haven't done that in a long time."

"Sure, Dad." *When was the last time he said that?* She studied his profile as he stood at the stove, watching the eggs fry. His face seemed more lined, like a dried cantaloupe. She hadn't noticed that his hair was thinner and grayer than she remembered. *It's been a long time since I've really looked at him. He is getting older. And more tired looking.*

She poured a cup of coffee and sat down at the table. Morgan set a plate with strips of beef and an egg in front of her. He removed the tray of biscuits from the oven and slid them onto a platter. As he set it down in front of her, she noticed how scarred and thick his hands had become. The knuckles swollen. *No wonder he rubs and pulls on his fingers.*

Morgan and Carolina got into the old ranch pickup and started for the first pasture. She could not find any words. The dread choked her. She stared out at the pasture. As they passed small gatherings of cattle, she turned to study them.

"You need to remember that the shinnery is bad in this pasture. Especially for the pregnant heifers. They will slough their calves. It'll poison cattle if they eat enough of it. I've been burning it ever year, but I can't get ahead of it."

"I know, Dad. That's why we move everything off of this pasture until the grass greens up."

"Good girl. You have been listening. Remember that the east fence gets buried with sand in the spring when the wind blows. In late spring it needs to be checked to be sure that everything is right. Be sure that the cattle can't get over it. If you keep the tumbleweeds off of it, the sand won't bank up so fast. Every few years I put up a new fence. It depends on how much the wind blows."

"Dad, why are we doing this? Are you dying?"

"No, Carolina. I am not, but I am serious about you taking over the running of this ranch."

"Dad, I know all this. What's happening?"

"Carolina, this is your ranch, and I won't always be around. I want to be sure that you know these things. Travis will help. So will Tom and Eldrige if you need them. Trust Travis. He knows this ranch and how to take care of it. And you," he added, glancing at her.

"Dad! I don't know if Travis and I will ever get back together. I can't depend on him."

"You can depend on him. Even if you don't get together. He will always be a good neighbor. And friend."

"Then what is it?"

"Carolina, you just need to pay close attention to what I say." Morgan drove to the horseshoe bend in The River. He sat there for a long time before getting out of the truck. "Come on. I want to show you something."

Carolina followed him to where he stood, dangerously close to the red riverbank, looking down. "Dad, why are we here? You always told me not come here, that it was dangerous."

"It is dangerous. And stay away from here. I just wanted to show you where I pulled your father out of The River when you were five. Do you remember?"

"Vaguely. Why do I have to see this again?"

"Because you need to remember."

She stared at him. *How strange. Is this what Mom meant when she said that Dad had secrets that he might tell her sometime?* A sense of foreboding filled her.

"A person is foolish to go into The River when it's running at flood stage. Your father got swept into a whirlpool. We both nearly drowned."

"I remember all that, Dad." She was getting vexed with him. *Is he babbling or did this have a purpose? What is he doing, reminding me of all this?*

"There are some things that you should notice. Look at these spider webs." He pointed to the webs, woven into the mesquite branches. "If the webs are high and loose like this, it means good weather. If they are close to the ground and tight, bad weather is coming. Heavy hair on the cattle means a bad winter."

Is he stalling? Is there something else? I need to get him away from here. "You taught me all of that years ago, Dad. Is there any other good advice for the day?" she said in an annoyed voice.

"Yes. A new broom sweeps clean and kiss your money so it will return to you."

"Oh, Dad."

"Let's get back." Morgan said.

That's it? That's why he called me out here? Irritated, Carolina silently followed him to the truck.

Carolina cleared the table and said, "I'll take care of the dishes if you have something else to do."

"I do need to mend a saddle. The leathers and tools are in the barn." Morgan set his hat on his head and stepped out the back door.

She watched him, noticing that his shoulders were not as straight as she remembered. He seemed to have something on his mind, but she knew that he would not confide in her until he had the details worked out. Her stomach churned with anxiety. *What was all that craziness yesterday? He seems better today but distracted.*

The morning was slipping away when she noticed Morgan in the front yard, tending to the lavender plants. "Dad, I need to go to the house for some things. Do you need anything in town?"

"Yes, I started a list. If you see anything else you want, get it. I don't usually have things like yogurt. The list is on the refrigerator. You need to come back when you're finished."

Morgan looked up at her, standing above him on the porch. His face held a sternness that she had never seen. They looked intently into each other's eyes before he bent to pull weeds from around the lavender plants.

She drove across the cattle guard and moved slowly down the road. A small herd of antelope loped along the fence, keeping time with her pick up. She rolled down the window to sniff the air. Her dad had always told her to tell the weather by looking and smelling. She pulled over and studied the pastures.

The winter grass seemed grayer than normal. And sparser. Most of the cattle had been moved to better feed. The yucca spears stabbed the faded winter sky with flowerless points. Even the rabbits were burrowing in for the winter. She watched a hawk circling, searching for something to eat in the bleak landscape.

Carolina reached to put the truck in gear and noticed a new billboard. She smiled. The road sign showed the picture of a state policeman with hand on hip. The words under him read, "Honestly now, what's your hurry? Slow down, drive safe."

She checked her rear-view mirror before pulling onto the road and saw that a sheriff's car had pulled up behind her, stopping some distance back. She turned off the motor and watched as Greg Carrasco stepped slowly from the car.

She studied him as he approached. He was watching her in the side mirror. Carolina could tell by his gait that he was satisfied with himself. *The little banty rooster. He has a new hat with a cattleman's crease. Right! He doesn't have shit, much less cattle. Just bullshit. Here he comes.* She rolled down the window and waited for him to sidle up. She composed her face, trying not to show what she thought of him.

"Well. Hello, Carolina. I noticed that you were parked out here. Anything wrong?"

"No. I was just looking at the pasture."

"Lookin' pretty bad, isn't it? I guess you'll have to start selling your cattle, soon."

"Dad has that handled. Not to worry."

An old Ford drove slowly by, the driver peering around to see who was getting a ticket. The car backfired. Carrasco ducked and spun around, pulling his gun. Carolina stifled a smile and said, "I guess you've been shot at before."

"In fact, I have," he said, turning to face her.

Too bad they missed, she thought.

Continuing his conversation, he said, "I wasn't worried. Just making small talk. I thought you might need some help changing a tire or something."

"Nope. I'm just fine."

"Good to hear. Say, I heard you were getting a divorce. How about you and me going out sometime. I could show you a really good time."

"No thanks. I'm not interested in dating right now."

"How do you know if you don't try me?"

"I know."

"Are you on the prod about something, Carolina?"

"No, Greg. I am not on the prod. I'm just not interested."

"We could have a cowboy wedding. You know, we say 'I do' over a bottle of beer and then spend the weekend together. We could go up to Santa Fe or something. Maybe get to know each other better, how about it?"

"Greg, we are as close as we are going to get."

"Close only counts in horseshoes and hand grenades, Carolina."

She took a slow breath, holding it as she swallowed the words that tried to escape her mouth. "Greg, are you going to give me a ticket? If not, I need to go."

"I could probably find something to ticket you for, but I won't. Give it some thought, Carolina. I make a pretty good date."

"I'll keep that in mind," she said, rolling up the window.

Chapter 23
The Revelation
2012

Morgan stood, hip shot, leaning against the door frame. shifting to ease the ache that always radiated from his right leg. The pain in his face seemed to come from somewhere deeper inside than the wounded leg would warrant. He studied Carolina, immersed in a book, seated at the kitchen table.

"Honey, come to the living room. We need to talk."

She lifted her head with an anxious look but said nothing as she searched his face, hoping to read some sign of what was on his mind. She rose. Morgan put a large, calloused hand on her shoulder and guided her to the sofa. He was silent as he watched her kick off her shoes and tuck her long legs up under her, reaching for a throw pillow to clutch against her abdomen. Hugging it for comfort.

She settled herself and then watched as he gingerly eased himself into the large, brown leather club chair that he favored. She sat across from him, this man who had raised her and loved her. He wanted to talk. It must be serious. She tried to stop the roll call of all the things she could imagine. *Was he sick, dying? Was he leaving? Maybe he had found someone. That can't be bad. Was something wrong with the ranch? He did call me 'girl.' That always makes me feel special and protected. I am his girl, his only girl, his only child for that matter.*

She studied his hands. The joints swollen with arthritis. She wondered if they hurt. He never complained. The scars and callouses were evidence of a cowman, a man who worked the ranch.

Trying to delay the dreaded conversation she asked, "Dad, why don't you wear gloves?"

He looked down at his hands, spreading his fingers, then clenching them. "Because I nearly lost a finger once, fixing fence. The wire snapped and caught in the glove. It wrapped around my hand and arm. If I hadn't had my fence pliers, it could have been bad. But that is not what I want to talk about."

Her heart stopped. He leaned forward and without preamble asked, "Carolina, do you remember when I first came to this ranch?"

"Vaguely, Dad. It seems like you've always been here."

Morgan sat stiff-backed in his easy chair, leaning forward, his large brown hands resting on his knees, clasping and unclasping. He cleared his throat and spoke in a hoarse tone, "Carolina, sometimes it's the small things that break your heart."

She nodded as though she understood but said nothing. Her eyes misted. He was a blur as she sat very still, waiting.

He continued when she offered no comment. "I was riding on the other side of The River looking for cattle when I heard someone calling for help. Your father had been out looking for strays. The bank collapsed and he went in to the water with his horse. He was in deep trouble. He was hung up in his saddle and the water was high. It had been running hard and was going down so quicksand was forming, right in the horseshoe bend of The River."

"The one you always told me to stay away from."

"Yes."

"When I found him, he was in a bad way. The water was pulling him and his horse under. I was able to get to him and cut him loose. My horse swam to shore and your father and I managed to make it to the bank. He had swallowed a lot of the muddy water and was coughing and vomiting."

"I remember that, Dad. I was screaming and you picked me up."

Morgan nodded and continued. "After I caught up my horse we started back to this ranch. I couldn't save his horse, he washed away. Your mom put your dad to bed and doctored him. She even took him to town to see the doctor. He was in the hospital, but there wasn't much that could be done. He lived for three days."

Tears welled up in Carolina's eyes, but she still said nothing, trying to pull up those bad childhood memories.

"Carolina, I knew I couldn't leave you two out here on this hard scrabble ranch by yourselves, so I stayed. I thought I was just going to stay for a while. but I had nowhere to go. I loved you so much as I watched you grow. Your mom and I got along so we got married. It worked out for all of us."

"I love you too, Dad."

"Carolina, I have something to tell you that you might find difficult to be-lieve."

Here it comes! What Mom was talking about. His secret. Oh, God!

"I didn't believe it at first but when your father and I pulled up on the bank of The River we were both here, in this time. I was on the other side in another time before I went into the water. I was in love with a woman over there. I don't know if I can get back to her, but I want to try."

Carolina stared at him in disbelief. *What! Is this the secret? Is he going crazy? Getting senile?*

"But Dad! This is crazy. How can you go across The River to another time?" She stared at him for some sign that he was teasing. *He would never joke like this. What's wrong with him? Maybe I can convince him to see a doctor. Maybe that's what he was doing in Doctor Frank's office. Maybe those old biddies were right. Maybe, maybe, maybe...*

"I know sweetheart. I didn't believe it when I was first told. An old man ex-plained it to me a little. I met him some time ago. Doroteo found him and told me about him. I rode down River to talk to him. His name is Charlie Dunn. He came across a few years before I did. He said that there are many who have come over."

"If that's true then why haven't more people done it, Dad? How come we haven't heard about this?"

"I think that some have. That's what the old man told me. I suspect that El-drige may be one of them, though he never said."

"Eldrige!? What makes you think he comes from the other side?"

"His ways. He's different."

"I have been studying up on this, Carolina. I don't understand completely but it has to do with electrical waves in the earth and when the water is circling very fast. I have tried to figure it out but it's above my pay grade. It has to do with Vectors and circulation."

Carolina sat in stunned silence, unable to grasp what he was saying. His face became a blur. Tears slid down her cheeks. Morgan stood and reached for her. She shrugged him off and hurried outside. She collapsed on the steps with her head in her hands. *Was he crazy!?*

Morgan stood in the doorway not knowing what to say or do. Tears welled in his eyes as he watched his daughter in pain, trying to come to grips with this situation.

He went to the kitchen and got the bottle of bourbon, mixed two drinks and went outside, carrying the bottle. Sitting down beside Carolina he silently handed her a drink.

He sat there, rolling the glass in his hands. He had hurt her. Frightened her. And still he could not explain to Carolina what had happened to him. Or why he needed to go back. "Sweetheart, I'm sorry. I waited as long as I could. I don't want to hurt you. Can you begin to understand just a little of what I'm trying to tell you and why?"

Wordless, she stared at him, seeing him as a stranger, not the father she had known. She shook her head, scared and confused.

"Your Mom has been gone for a long time and I keep thinking about Sophia. That's her name. I need to find out what happened to her. I can't help but think that if I can get back across The River she will be there."

"Dad, if this were true, then you nearly died. My father did. What makes you think that you can go back to another time?" She spoke slowly, trying to reason with him. Bring him back to sanity. It was hard to hear the words she was speaking over the pounding of her heart.

Morgan continued in a matter-of-fact tone, explaining. "I fell in love with her when I was in the army. She doctored me. Then I got a job working close to her dad's ranch. We were going to get married."

"What army?"

"The Confederate Army."

Carolina stared at him, her mouth open.

Morgan continued. "You're grown and things are looking good for you. I don't have much time left and I would like to spend it with her. The one thing about getting older, you have to choose the regrets that you can live with. Do you understand?"

Confederate Army! He sounds rational, like he really believes this. Is this what senility looks like?

Carolina sat silent, studying her dad. He seemed the same. But different. *What should I say? Maybe I should talk to Travis. Maybe he knows something. Maybe he can help. Again... Maybe, maybe, maybe.*

"If this is all true, when do you plan to leave?"

"When The River is red and running full."

She nodded, unable to find any words.

He waited.

She said nothing.

"My watch is ended. I stand relieved."

She puzzled at the old military term, unable to speak, not knowing what to say.

Chapter 24
The Crossing
2012———-1865

Morgan rode along The River, studying the roiling water. His stomach clenched with memories of how it felt that day. He took deep breaths, fighting down the fear. Could he withstand the shock of passing through again? Would she still be there? Would she still feel the same? Would he go back to the same time? He had decided that he didn't want to say goodbye again to the child he had raised. Let her grief be sudden. *If I see her again, I might not be able to say goodbye. It hurts too much to decide between Carolina and Sophia.* With his heart pounding, he touched his spurs to Buck's flanks, and they plunged into The River.

The roan struggled in the swirling currents. Rearing and plunging as he fought to stay upright. He screamed in pain. Morgan slipped out of the saddle, holding on to the horn in an effort to give the horse a better chance at staying afloat. He hoped that he could find some purchase in the muddy bottom. He stayed back of the thrashing front feet. He felt the same crushing sensation, the electrical current vibrating through his being. The roan must be feeling the same. As they were swept with the currents, he watched the trees slide by. Broken limbs slammed into them, bruising, scratching them both.

Morgan reached up and put his hand on the Buck's neck, speaking to him, patting him, giving him a comfort that he did not feel. Gradually, as they were removed from the swift eddies, the horse edged closer to the embankment. The horse gained footing in the mud and clamored up the embankment, dragging Morgan beside him. Morgan fell to the ground, breathless and in pain from the residual shock. His heart hurt from the electrical current which had run through it. The roan stood over him trembling and groaning. There was no way for Morgan to determine how long they stayed like that.

It hurt much more than the first time he had done this. He lay there, with the horse hovering over him until the sky turned grey. He stood and took an unsteady step, slowly leading the roan away from The River. He unsaddled and hobbled the horse and found a place among the trees to bed down. *Well, old boy, one step closer to Sophia.*

Morgan woke with the sun and took stock of his situation. He would have to put the damp blanket back on the horse. That won't work for very long. The soggy saddle was uncomfortable. The horse was fractious and hard to handle. They were both hungry.

He spent the day riding, heading in the direction of where Randel's ranch used to be. His clothes had dried on him, stiff and rubbing sores in his skin. Morgan knew that the horse probably had saddle sores.

He dismounted and pulled the saddle off. Grabbing handfuls of dry grass, he began to groom the horse, gently avoiding the sores. He rubbed grass in his own hair trying to get rid of the mud. He pulled off his clothes and pulled another set from his saddle bags. They were soggy but were not caked with mud. He spread them on the ground and sat down to let them air dry. The air was cool.

Morgan lay back and dozed. He was awakened by the sound of hooves. Sitting up, he was surprised to see a rider coming at a lope. He stood and waited, aware of the sight he must present. The young cowboy looked vaguely familiar. He reined up and put his hand on the rifle butt where it nestled in the scabbard, under his leg.

"Evening. What's going on here?" the horseman asked.

"Evening. I may be lost. Can you tell me where I am?"

"Where are you supposed to be." The young man countered. He looked Morgan up and down, taking in the hobbled horse, the clothes spread out to dry on the ground and the nearly naked man standing before him in underwear and a pair of socks.

"I'm looking for the Randel place."

The young man urged his horse nearer and reached down with his hand. "You found it. I'm Josh Randel."

Chapter 25
The Search
2012

Carolina watched as the truck approached the house. She studied Travis as he unloaded his horse and slowly walked him to the corral. His shoulders were hunched like the weight of all this was on him as well.

She pulled down the Crown Royal from the cabinet and filled two glasses, topping them off with Seven Up.

He tapped lightly on the door and opened it slowly, looking for her. She handed him a glass and slid into his arms. Dry, wracking sobs shook her shoulders. He held her tight, not wanting her to see the tears in his eyes. The loss of his friend and the pain in Carolina were more than he could deal with now. He led her to the sofa and laid back so she could rest on his chest. They emptied their glasses and sat, silent.

Travis woke from a nap to find Carolina asleep on his lap. He sat still, gently touching her hair, studying her tear-streaked face. She stirred and raised her head, looking at him, uncomprehending. He watched as the realization of her loss flooded her face. Tears welled up in her eyes.

"Cee, you're going to be alright. I'm here for you, always. We'll get through this."

"Travis, did Dad ever talk to you about going across to the other side of The River?"

He studied her, wondering how much Morgan had told her. "What do you mean?"

"I mean, did he tell you that he came from another time and wanted to go back?"

"Yes. Not long before he left. It sounded preposterous to me at the time. I have since talked to my Quantum Physics professor at the college and he gave me some books to read on my own. There have been some earth electrical wave studies done. Mostly in Colorado, by Feynman and Tesla. It still seems pretty farfetched but there is so much that we don't know. Maybe they were on to something."

"How am I going to make it without him, Travis? I can't do this alone."

He cradled her face in his hands. "You don't have to do this alone, Carolina."

"But where is he, Travis?"

He shook his head. "I don't know. I just don't know. Maybe he was right and he did go back. If he did, I hope he found what he was looking for. There's been something gnawing at him for as long as I've known him."

"That's what Mom said. She knew there was something but he never told her what it was."

"Maybe because he didn't know that he could do anything about it before now."

"How can I find out? Where do I start looking?"

"I think when things settle down, we should have a talk with Doroteo. Find out exactly where this Charlie Dunn is. That's where your dad started."

"Are you going to help me, Travis?" He tilted her face up to be kissed. "Of course, sweetheart."

<u>**Local Rancher Missing**</u>

Prominent local rancher, Morgan
Donnally was reported missing on
Friday by his daughter. Last seen at
his ranch. Friends and neighbors are
horseback, riding The River.
Donnally was known for his
generosity and ranching innovations.
The deep water and swift currents are
hindering the search. At this time it is
not known if he went across to the
Other Side of The River

About the Author

After spending her youth on Southern California beaches, she moved to New Mexico where she finished her education and began her working career in the field of Interior Design. This endeavor allowed her to pursue her real love-Ranching. Her many years in the ranching business lends authenticity to her writing. When she writes about branding, building fences, working cattle, and all other aspects of ranching she knows what she is writing about. She has done it all. She lived in New Mexico for many years before retiring to Tennessee where she continues to write and enjoy her family and gardening. She has published The Other Side of The River and is at work on a prequel. She also has an anecdotal book about the tribulations of being a landlord in New Mexico in the works. She brings her life experiences to her writing.

About the Publisher